To:
Vivian
From:
Granny

Christmas 2019

To:
Vivian
From:
Granny
Christmas 2014

HENRY HUNTER

HENRY HUNTER

AND THE BEAST OF SNAGOV

JOHN MATTHEWS

Sky Pony
New York

Sky Pony Press books may be purchased in bulk at special discounts for sales promotion, corporate gifts, fund-raising, or educational purposes. Special editions can also be created to specifications. For details, contact the Special Sales Department, Sky Pony Press, 307 West 36th Street, 11th Floor, New York, NY 10018 or info@skyhorsepublishing.com.

Sky Pony® is a registered trademark of Skyhorse Publishing, Inc.®, a Delaware corporation.

Visit our website at www.skyponypress.com.

10 9 8 7 6 5 4 3 2 1

Library of Congress Cataloging-in-Publication Data is available on file.

Cover design by Mina Bach
Interior design by Will Steele
Illustrations by Nick Tankard

Print ISBN: 978-1-5107-1038-2
Ebook ISBN: 978-1-5107-1041-2

Printed in the United States of America

*To Robin Berk, who is more like
Henry Hunter than anyone I know.*

PROLOGUE

HOW I MET
HENRY HUNTER

The first time I saw Henry Hunter he was hanging by his fingertips from the windowsill of the principal's office.

He looked down as I walked past, fixing me with his large, slightly protuberant blue eyes and said, "Could you spare a moment, old chap?"

(Yes, he really does talk like that.)

I wasn't really sure whether to answer or just ignore the boy dangling from the window. You see, I hadn't been at St. Grimbold's School for Extraordinary Boys very long, and wasn't sure of the protocol in such an event. But he did look as though he might fall at any moment.

"Um, can I help?" I asked.

"Well, could you be a good fellow and fetch the ladder from the gardener's shed?" said Henry, beaming at me.

The gardener's shed was just a short walk away, but since the situation seemed to call for it I ran all the way there and back. I leaned the ladder against the wall, angling it close enough for Henry to reach with his feet and climb down.

"Thanks!" he said rather breathlessly. Then he nodded towards the window of the principal's office and added, "You might be better off not hanging around here for a while."

"Okay...right...thanks," I said, wondering what I was thanking him for. I found myself following Henry as he walked quickly away across the playing fields. He headed towards the elm trees that lined the drive up to the imposing cast iron school gates.

I caught up with Henry and noticed he had a bundle of bright green cloth tucked into the front of his school blazer.

"So—um—what were you doing up there, anyway?" I ventured. I didn't normally ask such direct questions, but somehow I knew the answer would be too intriguing to ignore.

Henry turned his bright blue eyes on me. "I'm not sure you'd believe me if I told you," he said.

"Try me," I answered. I was becoming intrigued by Henry's odd behavior and the way he spoke.

"Okay," said Henry. He looked around

to make sure no one was watching, then pulled the mysterious bundle from his jacket, unwrapping the fabric at the edge for me to see what was inside. It looked a bit like a flute—but not the kind likely to be played in a school orchestra. This one was elaborately carved out of what looked like old bone (not, I hoped, human—but you never know).

I didn't know what to say. "I-I've never seen anything like it before!" I stuttered.

"That's not surprising," said Henry, pushing back his slightly floppy hair, "because it's one of a kind. Anyone who listens to it has to do whatever the person blowing it says! I didn't think it was the sort of thing Dr. Hossenfeffer should be in charge of."

There it was. The sort of casual remark I became very familiar with as I got to know Henry Hunter better. The sort that showed that he, a twelve-year-old (even in a school for extraordinary boys), thought nothing of challenging the principal. I'd soon discover that it was the kind of thing Henry Hunter did all the time.

Henry explained that Dr. Hossenfeffer, the current headmaster of St. Grimbold's, had stolen the strange flute from a passing Himalayan priest. I suspect his reason may have had something to do with trying to control a hundred and fifty unusual boys, but in any case Henry had decided it was far too powerful an object to be in the hands of an ordinary principal—especially one who was supposed to be looking after us. So he'd picked the lock of Professor Hossenfeffer's study, cracked the seven codes required to open the principal's lock box, taken the flute, and was just about to leave when he heard the old boy coming. That's when he climbed out of the window and found he was stuck. I came along and the rest, as they say, is history.

After the whole dangling-from-the-window-ledge event Henry and I became best friends. Although I'm not quite sure why. Maybe it's because every hero needs a sidekick—or at least someone to tell the story of their adventures. Since then, Henry has said to me on more than one occasion: "Every Sherlock Holmes needs his Watson, Dolf, and you are mine."

I had at first thought this wasn't very flattering—everyone knows Dr. Watson isn't the sharpest knife in the box—but I soon came to realize that almost no one is as bright as Henry Hunter, so I decided I could live with the comparison.

A few days after the incident of the flute, Henry came up to me in the quad and said in his rather high and nasal voice, "You're Adolphus Pringle, aren't you?"

I nodded, a bit surprised he knew my name—I hadn't mentioned it during the windowsill rescue.

"I just wanted to thank you for helping me out of trouble the other day," Henry said, flashing me a toothy grin.

"You're welcome," I told him. "It was no problem."

Henry and I stood in the corner of the quad, quiet for a moment—one of those rather awkward silences that sometimes happen when no one can think of what to say next.

Then Henry grinned again and said, "Listen, I'm just off to look for this rare bug. Like to come along?"

Looking back, I don't know whether he

really wanted me to come along or if it was just something to say, but that didn't occur to me then and I jumped at the opportunity of doing something other than school lessons or homework. Of course he neglected to tell me that the bug he was looking for was a foot long and only found in the jungles of Africa, but that was Henry for you. I also didn't know he'd charted a Learjet, hired some local natives as guides, and that he was carrying a $30,000 video camera with which he intended to capture it on film.

As we tore through the skies at 50,000 feet in the Learjet, Henry explained that everything strange about his life began with his name. Having the surname Hunter got him interested in hunting for things—but not for just anything, like a great new sandwich or a book by his favorite author—but BIG THINGS, like legendary creatures and items that no one believed in, such as aliens, the yeti, the Holy Grail, mummies, and the crown of Alexander the Great. At first it meant looking stuff up in books (Henry always did that instead of using the Internet—which he said made you lazy) but in time he graduated to mounting actual expeditions in search of particular things.

He could afford to do this and things like hiring the Lear, because his parents were rich—his dad had, years ago, invented the Cronos microchip, which revolutionized the gaming industry by making it possible for gamers to interact with their favorite characters more closely than ever before. Then he'd created the *Cronopticon* (voted Best Games Machine Ever for several years running) and after that the *Cronopticon 2*, the *Cronopticon Gigantic* and the *Cronopticon Mini*—until just about everyone in the world owned one of his consoles. His dad was clever—but not as clever as Henry who, by the time he was ten, had degrees in subjects most people have never even heard of. Astrophysics, lepidoptera, and callisthenics are some of the ones I can remember.

Henry also told me that he could disappear on adventures like this because his parents weren't around. His mother had suddenly got a bad attack of responsibility and decided that she and her husband should put their billions to good use. They were off in search of a particularly rare orchid, which it was rumored could cure half the diseases in the world. At first they came home every month or so to see Henry, but after a bit all he saw of them was an occasional email and a video call on his birthday and Christmas.

So that was how Henry had ended up at St. Grimbold's, which may sound a bit tough on him, but he said he liked having parents who were off doing something useful and exciting—and it meant he had the kind of freedom no one gets when they're twelve.

I didn't have much of an opportunity to tell Henry about my background. Which is just as well, because I'm not super bright, and I don't have an upper-class accent or designer clothes or any of that stuff. I just happen not to fit too well in the kind of school that insists on homework, the right kind of gym bag, and shirts properly tucked in. My last principal told me, "Pringle, you have an overactive imagination. It is not welcome here." Luckily St. Grimbold's has a trust fund to offer scholarships to kids like me, who are reasonably smart but whose parents are anything but rich, to get "a proper education," as my dad calls it.

The Hunters were another matter; they forked over a pretty hefty sum to get Henry into St. Grimbold's, and they made it pretty easy for Henry to indulge in his hobby.

Hunting.

You name it: Henry hunted it.

And most of the time, I was with him.

The rare bug adventure was actually pretty ordinary compared to some we've had since, though we did encounter a group of hunters who were just as keen as Henry to find the bug, and who were prepared to do anything to stop us. But, thanks to Henry's amazing skill and encyclopedic knowledge of lepidoptera, we managed to escape, and film the giant bug, without getting killed. But that's a story for another time.

For now, I want to start with a different adventure, one that's more important for you to know about. A story that still gives me goosebumps. Not The Story of the Great Lizard of Jambalaya, or The Adventure of The Curried Frogs. It's one from Henry's files, an adventure that I think might contain some vital clues about Henry that I need rather badly. Of course I was there, so I know what happened, but, dear reader, I need your help.

So please keep your eyes peeled, your ear to the ground, your mouth wide. Because this is the first of . . .

THE HENRY HUNTER FILES:

THE BEAST OF SNAGOV

Of Course There Are Vampires, Dolf...

This particular adventure started the way many of them did, with Henry Hunter sitting in the only comfortable chair in his study at St. Grimbold's—a swiveling leather recliner. His feet were up on the desk and he was reading the latest issue of his favorite magazine—*The Unbelievable Times: A Journal of Unlikely Events and Strange Prognostications*. I thought it was mostly a load of garbage, and told Henry as much, but he swore it was the best source of information on almost everything strange going on in the world. For instance, I remember the story of "The Martian Pyramids," and "The Man Who Transferred his Brain to a Chipmunk." But as the *Unbelievable Times* had fuelled more than one of our adventures, I couldn't really argue.

"Listen to this, Dolf!" he said as I came back from the school shop, balancing two large milkshakes and a bag of candy in my arms. Pushing back his floppy hair, he read from the magazine.

DRACULA—A REAL-LIFE VAMPIRE?

Professor Killigrew, of the British Museum, has this week uncovered some missing papers that could prove the existence of Dracula—and that he was not just a figment of the author Bram Stoker's imagination. Incomplete papers found in a cellar of a London house, thought to be written by Stoker's publisher, includes the passage:

"A number of people have spoken to me regarding the events in Mr. Stoker's novel. It seems I am not the only person to believe that they are no mere fiction, but actually an account of real events. The implications of this for the world are frightening, since they imply that such creatures as the Dreadful Count really do exist. Are any of us safe from them, I wonder? I must confess that I am almost sorry to have published the book at all, though its success has far exceeded my expectations. The only possible explanation for the events of the last few weeks is that one of the Creatures still exists. I cannot begin to say how terrible this would be if it is true. I have spoken with Mr. Stoker and I can see that he, too, is afraid. I have taken the advice of several men of learning and they have suggested that I should conceal the location of the Beast lest it be discovered and somehow set free. Such an event is beyond anything I could imagine."

However, Professor Killigrew, when pressed, would not suggest there is any truth in the words. "It's an interesting find, and our tests do show that it was written back in the late 19th century. But it is more likely to be an elaborate hoax. The references to 'beasts' and 'creatures' are pure nonsense, of course. I think it a trick to sell more copies of the book!"

But when we spoke to a Dracula expert, Professor Hans Trembling, from Whitby, he said, "There is indisputable evidence that vampires existed—indeed that they do still exist. This new evidence could be hugely important."

"What do you make of that?" Henry asked.

"Sounds like a load of garbage," I said, sipping my milkshake. "Wasn't Dracula killed, anyway?"

"Only in a few old horror films," said Henry. "Or maybe in that Hollywood movie— what was it called—*Van Helsing?*"

"I liked that film," I said. "Great CGI. So you're telling me Dracula was a real person? That vampires exist?"

"Of course there are vampires, Dolf!" answered Henry. "There's plenty of information going back hundreds of years that tells us they really existed. Vlad Tepes— aka Vlad the Impaler—was the most famous, and that's who Stoker based his book on. . . ."

He fell silent for a moment, staring into space with a familiar gleam in his eyes.

"Does this mean we'll be going to Transylvania?" I knew that much about Dracula, at least. Although I had no idea

where Transylvania was, I had a feeling we wouldn't be back for dinner.

Henry Hunter beamed. "Almost certainly, Dolf, but something tells me we should go to Whitby first."

Before I had time to finish Henry's milkshake, we were on our way to Whitby. As our train whistled though the "picturesque" countryside (according to the tourism ad at the end of our carriage), heading northeast, Henry gave me a short lesson in the history of Bram Stoker, Whitby, and vampires. (In fact, it was a rather long lecture, since the journey lasted three hours, but here are the interesting bits.)

"Bram—short for Abraham—Stoker was born in Ireland in 1847. He wrote *Dracula* after visiting Whitby in 1890. Did you know

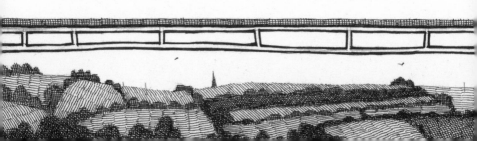

he was going to call it by a far more catchy
title: *The Un-dead*? There are all kinds of
theories about where he got the idea from.
Some say he borrowed a library book about
the places where vampires are supposed to
live. The *Unbelievable Times* ran an article once
saying that a weird old guy called Arminius
Vambery had told Bram about 'strange
goings on' in Whitby while he was sitting on
the cliffs overlooking the sea."

"So he stole the story?" I asked, disappointed by the possibility that not even Bram
Stoker was original.

"Possibly—we don't know." Henry shrugged.
"Anyway, Bram stayed for a day or two in
the town and then went off to write his book.
He came back a few times after that and ever
since Whitby has been known as the home

of Dracula—even though the Count actually never stayed there in the book. He just came ashore there from a ship carrying his coffin full of earth and went on to London. That's where most of the story takes place."

"But if he was never really there, why are we going to Whitby?" Not that I didn't want to be there—it was better than being in school any day! Luckily for me, Henry had managed to convince the school board—and my parents, who were a bit in awe of him— that I would learn a lot more if I went with him on his various "field trips."

"Because I think there's more to find out about Bram Stoker and his book. Always go to the source, Dolf."

"So what kind of thing are we looking for?" I was trying to figure out how I might be of help here.

"You mean apart from Dracula?" said

Henry with a grin. "Probably papers of some kind."

"Oh," I said, trying not to show my disappointment. There always seemed to be dusty old papers involved in Henry's adventures.

"Well, the first thing is to talk to the 'local expert' from the *Unbelievable Times* article. He certainly seems to believe in vampires." It's not surprising Bram Stoker chose Whitby as the setting for Dracula's arrival in England. The town hangs on to the cliffs like a dog biting the hem of a long coat, shivering from the battering winds and waves of the North Sea. Over it all looms Whitby Abbey, a great ruin of a place believed to be haunted by the ghosts of long-dead nuns—though I never saw a single one while we were there. In short, it's bleak, chilly, and the kind of place that gives me the creeps. I had to fight the

urge to look over my shoulder for monsters every five minutes.

From the station we headed to the offices of the local newspaper, where Henry, with his usual charm, persuaded the receptionist to give us the address of Dr. Hans Trembling.

We walked through the narrow streets of the town center—which looked really ordinary for somewhere with such a weird reputation for . . . well, weirdness—and less than fifteen minutes later we were knocking on the front door of a small, rather neglected house. Paint peeled from the door and window frames, and the curtains were drawn, but a brass plate to one side of the door declared it to be the home of

DR. H. S. TREMBLING PhD

Without hesitation, Henry knocked confidently on the door. We waited for a few minutes—longer than was normal, I had started to think. But then Henry knocked again, louder this time. Still no one came.

"Must be out," I remarked.

"Maybe . . ." said Henry. He stood back and scanned the windows on the upper floor. The curtains were drawn up there, too.

"Or he might have gone away."

"I don't think so," Henry replied. "Notice how shiny that brass plate is. It's been cleaned recently. Besides, he was quoted in the *Unbelievable Times* article just a few days ago, so he can't have been gone that long."

As always, I was impressed by Henry's sleuthing skills.

Henry shook his head. "There's something not right about this, Dolf."

I sighed. We'd been in Whitby less than an hour, and we'd already come to the end of our investigation. I looked at my watch,

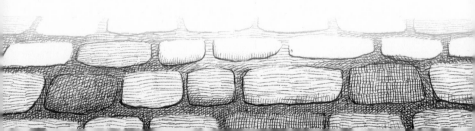

hoping we wouldn't get back to school in time for double math.

"Let's see what the neighbors have to say," Henry said. I should have known Henry would never give up that easily.

We tried knocking on a couple of doors. The first was opened by a short, fat man who took one look at us and slammed the door in our faces. At the second door there was no answer. The third was opened by a pleasant, elderly lady. By her quick eyes and sharp tongue I could tell right away she was the type of person who likes to sit all day and watch the world go by, and hence knows everything that happens.

"Dr. Trembling?" she said, after Henry had posed his question. "Funny you should ask that, young man. Another gentleman was looking for him just yesterday."

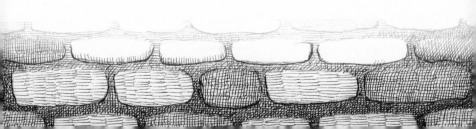

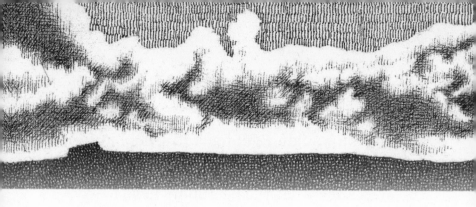

"Really?" Henry said innocently. "What did he look like?"

"Let's see now—tall, thin . . . quite pale about the face, like he doesn't see the sun much. Spoke with a bit of a foreign accent . . . very polite, though."

"What were you able to tell him . . . about Dr. Trembling, I mean?" said Henry.

"I saw the professor getting into a car two—no, wait, I tell a lie, three days ago. Came quite late, it did. Stood outside the house for about an hour. Then I saw Professor Trembling get in. He seemed uneasy on his feet—like he wasn't well—but it was dark by then so I can't be sure."

"I don't suppose you remember which way it went?" Henry asked.

The old lady's eyes gleamed. "Why yes, as a matter of fact I do." Clearly it was a point of pride that our informant hadn't missed anything. "It went off that way." She pointed up the narrow street, which climbed towards the looming mass of Whitby Abbey.

Henry beamed. "Thank you so much," he said. "You've been very helpful."

She returned his smile and waved as we headed off up the road. Was she wondering why two schoolboys were asking after Dr. Hans Trembling? Although it has to be said that Henry didn't look like most twelve-year-old boys. Today he wore a black fedora and a suit tailored at the famous Saville Row. I, on the other hand, in case you're interested, was wearing an old pair of jeans and a Metallica

T-shirt (I like that retro stuff—okay?).

"What now?" I asked as we trudged up the steep street.

"Well, something's going on, that's for sure," said Henry. "I'll bet whoever took the professor away in that car was up to no good."

"What about the foreign bloke who asked about him yesterday?" I didn't want to mention that the elderly lady had pretty much described most people's idea of Dracula— everything except the teeth and long black cloak, that was.

"May or may not be connected," said Henry. "And it could be as a result of the article. But it sounds like the people who were after Dr. Trembling were also being followed."

"So what's next?"

Henry quickened his pace, striding off in front of me up the hill. "I think its time we visited Bram Stoker."

An Encounter With Some Unpleasant People

I wasn't sure how we were going to meet the author of *Dracula*, since Bram Stoker had been dead for ages, but I followed Henry up the steep narrow streets anyway, climbing above the red roofs of the old town until we reached a crescent-shaped row of houses. Henry produced a map from his pocket, on which he traced the way to a symbol marking where Bram Stoker had stayed in Whitby.

The exact house was easy to spot—it had one of those blue plaques telling you someone famous had lived there.

"It's a bit . . . ordinary," I said, looking up at the tall, narrow townhouse.

"Expecting a Gothic mansion with blood running down the walls?" laughed Henry. "Just wait—it's usually the places that look the most ordinary that have the most extraordinary things inside."

Henry knocked on the door, but no one answered, so he bent down and looked though the mail box.

"It's empty," I heard him mumble into the door.

"That's that, then," I said, turning back down the steps.

"Don't be silly, Dolf. We have to get inside. Anyway, it's not this part of the house we want to get into, it's the part no one knows about."

"If no one knows about it, how come you do?" I said. I don't know why I asked this really—Henry knew a lot more about most things than most other people!

Henry raised his eyebrows whilst already looking around for another way in—though since the house was sandwiched between two others I couldn't see how it'd be possible.

While I was wondering this, Henry was already pushing his way behind a large bush in front of the house. "Here we go, Dolf!" he said. "Come on!"

Glancing around to make sure there was no one watching, I squeezed in behind the bush and saw what he had found. It was a narrow, horizontal window in the basement of the house.

The glass was already cracked and before I could question him Henry had smashed a stone into it, reached in and opened the catch. He pushed the window up and climbed though.

Before I could change my mind, I followed Henry, feet first, and found myself standing in a dark, dusty basement. A dirty light bulb, which I was surprised still worked when Henry flicked a switch, cast a dim glow over the room. It was completely empty apart from clusters of cobwebs and a lot of dust. Henry was standing by a warped, peeling door, which he had already opened. Beyond lay only darkness.

Henry produced a slim flashlight from his pocket and shone it into the gloom. All we could see was a flight of narrow stairs leading down into even darker regions.

"Um, any idea what's down there?" I asked, unable to stop myself thinking of people with long, snaggly teeth.

"Hopefully the answers to some questions," replied Henry, and set off down the stairs. I jumped to follow him before his light disappeared completely.

Five minutes later we were still descending, occasionally twisting right and left. The walls had turned from stone to just bare earth. A strong smell of damp and something else unpleasant I couldn't identify permeated the air.

"How much further do you think this goes?" I asked. My voice echoed back at us from every side.

"No idea," said Henry. Then he grunted and muttered, "Ah-ha!" in a meaningful way.

"Ah-ha, what?" Had the monsters appeared already?

"We're not going down any longer," answered Henry.

"It feels like we are," I said as I felt for the next step with my foot.

"Yes, that's the trick of it," said Henry, pulling out a compass and shining his flashlight on it. "It's like those theme park rides where you think you've been on and on for ages but you've just been doubling back on yourself. This is really interesting."

I wasn't sure how it was that interesting, but I didn't like to say anything. I was more worried about the cold and damp, which were by now making me shiver, and Henry's flashlight was beginning to dim.

I was wondering how much longer we'd be going on for when Henry stopped so suddenly I bumped into him.

"What?" I shouted, clutching the earthen wall to steady myself. Peering over Henry's shoulder I saw that he had stopped because there was a wall in front of him. The stairway ended there, with no sign of a door.

"Now what?" I said. "Should we dig through?" I patted my pocket, thinking that my Swiss army knife wouldn't get us very far.

Henry didn't answer. He shone his flickering flashlight around the narrow space, pushing his hair back from his eyes "This can't be it . . ." he muttered. Then he shone the flashlight upwards and grunted. I looked at the light and saw the outlines of a trapdoor in the ceiling.

"Come on then, Dolf," said Henry. "Give me a hand up."

Henry was soon expertly climbing through the trapdoor from my shoulders, and then reaching down to pull me up after him. He had surprising strength for someone with so little apparent muscle.

It was a

bit less dark here; a round and very grimy window let in a few gleams of evening sunlight (*Math class is long over*, I thought with a grin). We were in a small square room that seemed to have no other entrance or exit than the trapdoor. What it did have was a large wooden box fastened with a rusted lock in the middle of the room. Henry stood by it, visibly shaking with excitement. This is how he gets when one of his hunting expeditions leads to something real.

"This is it, Dolf," he said, his voice breaking a bit.

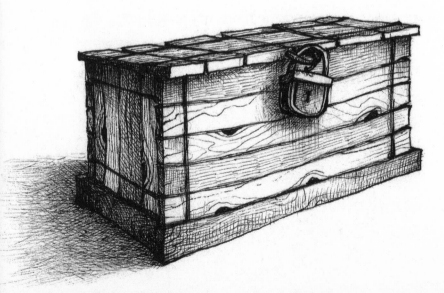

"What do you think's in there?" I asked. I had no idea what Henry was expecting—or hoping—for.

Henry was already on his knees, pushing at the lid.

It didn't budge.

Reaching into an inner pocket Henry brought out a small crowbar (this early on in our adventures I was still amazed by what he carried around with him) and pushed it under the lock. He levered it up and it gave at once.

With trembling hands Henry lifted the lid.

I sniffed—a peculiar smell, musty and sweetish, wafted from the box, and I peered over his shoulder as he shone his flashlight inside.

I couldn't help feeling rather disappointed when all I saw was a small bundle wrapped up in what looked like oilskin—the kind of stuff they make sailors' jackets out of.

Henry bent down and pulled it out. He sat back on his heels and held the bundle in his hands. His face was smudged and there were cobwebs in his hair, but his eyes were gleaming. I wanted to tell Henry to get on with it, to find out what was inside, but I knew how he liked to draw out dramatic moments, and now was no exception. Slowly he unwrapped the bundle and extracted an old, battered wooden box— it looked like the kind that holds cigars. He held it up towards the light and we could just make out a name engraved into the lid.

JONATHAN
HARKER

Even I gasped at that. Jonathan Harker is one of the main characters in Dracula, who went to the Count's castle in Transylvania.

"But he's a made-up character!" I said, my brain working overtime to figure out what was going on. "How come there's a box with his name on it?"

"Let's find out, shall we?" Henry said.

Inside the cigar box was a bundle of papers and what looked like a small, green glass bottle. Henry held this up for a moment, turning it this way and that to try to catch the light. Shaking his head he laid it to one side and began sifting though the documents. Were these linked to the papers found at the British Museum? I wondered.

"This is it, Dolf," Henry said, sitting back on his heels. "The real thing. There's another note from the publisher, Frederick Walker."

"What does it say?"

Henry held the yellowing paper close to his face and read it out loud.

"Here I have laid the writings upon which Mr. Stoker based his tale. When he brought his manuscript to me I had no idea that there was a real person by the name Jonathan Harker, or indeed that the terrible, accursed being of which he wrote was also real. I cannot allow this to become public knowledge lest it cause widespread panic. Though I am assured by Mr. Van Helsing that the devil is dead, there are too many things that suggest he may yet rise again."

Henry stopped and stared into space for a moment. "So not only was Jonathan Harker real but Abraham Van Helsing as well."

"I'll bet there are some people in Hollywood who would love to know that," I said, grinning.

Henry didn't seem to hear me. He raised the paper again and continued reading.

"Of far greater concern is the possible existence of the Snagov Beast. If the rumors are only half true, this is a more terrible creature than Dracula himself, or indeed any other vampire that has walked this earth. I have done my utmost to hide the whereabouts of the dreadful creature, just as I must now hide this account of the visit to Castle Dracula by Jonathan Harker himself.

Signed on this day of December the 21st 1899,

Frederic Walker, Esq.

"So now we know," said Henry.

"Um . . . what exactly do we know?" I said, wishing I had Henry's grasp of details and found it easier to keep up.

"It's simple enough, Dolf. Everything Bram Stoker wrote in his book was real. It actually happened. All those weird things he saw, the undead. It's all real."

"But that was all a long time ago," I put in.

"Yes, but there's something far more important here than the fact that vampires exist. I always thought they did anyway. It's this other creature, much more terrible than a vampire according to Frederick Walker, Esq., that I want to find out about. The Snagov Beast, that's what we should be hunting!"

"But what do you think it is?" I asked. I was trying to work out whether the move from vampires to beasts was a good one or not.

"Well, if it's worse than Dracula then it might be connected to the origin of all vampires. And that, my dear Dolf, is something we can't ignore. We absolutely have to hunt down the Snagov Beast."

"So now we go to Transylvania?" I said. There was no point trying to persuade him otherwise. Once Henry Hunter got that look in his eyes there was no turning back.

"Right you are, Dolf. But first we have to read this manuscript."

As Henry began to untie the piece of ribbon tied around the bundle of papers my eyes went back to the bottle he had laid to one side.

"What do you think's in that?" I asked.

Henry stopped what he was doing and picked up the bottle again.

"I'm not sure," he said, shaking it. "Doesn't seem to be anything inside at all."

"Why would Frederick Walker leave an old glass bottle in there?" I wondered. "Maybe it was part of his lunch."

"Well, I can tell you one thing," said Henry, ignoring my attempt at wit. "It's Transylvanian glass. Rather a nice specimen, in fact."

"Um, what's so special about Transylvanian glass?" I asked, hoping my question didn't generate another lecture.

"Oh, it's famous," beamed Henry. "They

47

use a special kind of technique. . . ." His words trailed off as he held the bottle up to the dim light filtering in through the window.

At that moment, with perfect timing, a ray of sunlight broke though the clouds. It struck the glass bottle full on and lit it up as if something inside had burst into flame. Henry gasped and I saw that he was staring at the wall across the room. Where the sunlight struck the bottle it had thrown a pattern onto the wall as if onto a screen. I could make out a series of what might have been letters, though they made no sense to me.

"It's writing," said Henry, "in old Romanian." (Was there no end to his knowledge? That made at least ten weird languages he knew.)

"What does it say?" I asked.

"Hang on . . . I'm a bit rusty, but I think it's . . . *In the . . . cleft . . .* yes, *In the cleft of the Mountain of the Worm is . . . the Snagov Beast.*"

Henry was silent for a moment, then he said. "There's another word here, Dolf. . . ." After the smallest of pauses he delivered it with relish. "*Beware.*"

As he said the word I suddenly felt cold. Maybe it was because the sun went behind a cloud, returning the room to its former dimness, but it seemed more than that. I shivered in spite of myself.

It was then that we heard a thump behind us and jumped. Spinning round we saw a dark figure emerging from the trapdoor. The only feature I could make out was a flash of eyes. Apart from that, the figure was clad entirely in black.

My first thought was one of relief that it was at least human. My second thought was less coherent as the figure leapt into the room and pounced on Henry, snatching the bundle of papers from him so quickly that he had no time to react. When he did, it was the usual HH response to this kind of thing. He planted a couple of quick karate blows to his opponent's midsection and swiped the legs from under him. (Henry was proficient in several kinds of unarmed combat.)

At the same time Henry threw me the glass bottle, which I caught and stuffed into a front pocket of my jeans. Our attacker had managed to keep hold of the precious bundle of pages, and scrambled back to his feet. I recoiled as he landed several quick punches on Henry's torso, felling him to the floor.

Other than Henry's small groans as he took the hits, all of this took place in complete silence. Spurred into action by the sight of Henry on the floor, I jumped our attacker, but he was too fast for me and began raining punches on me from all sides. Somehow I managed to stay standing, using my arms to block the blows, until he ended with a swift kick to my stomach. The next thing I knew I was flat on the floor, gasping for air.

I looked over at Henry, who was staggering upright once more, but something else caught my eye: a second figure appearing though the trapdoor. All in black like the first, this one was carrying nunchukus.

Henry had spotted him too. "Dolf. Follow me!"

I expected him to head for the trapdoor but instead he leaped towards the small round window and pulled out his crowbar. He hurled it, shattering the glass as the iron bar vanished through the window. Seconds later Henry dived through it and I followed, not stopping to worry what was on the other side—I figured it couldn't be any worse than the two attackers.

There was a brief rush of air as I fell, and I remember yelling "Aaaaagh!" as I wondered if it was all up for Henry and me. But I hit

the ground quickly and for the second time that day found myself gasping for breath. As I lay there I took in my surroundings: the earth on which I'd landed was actually quite soft and only a foot below the round window. By whatever strange route the underground passage had taken, it had somehow brought us out near the bottom of a cliff face, and we'd emerged from a ramshackle hut that had been built into the rock itself.

I caught a brief flash of a ski mask-covered face staring down at us from the smashed window before Henry's face replaced it as he bent over me, asking anxiously if I was okay.

"Been better," I said with a grin. "Who are those people?"

"Probably the same people who took Dr. Trembling," said Henry, offering me a hand up. "But they got what they came for anyway."

I should have realized that, I thought to myself. For not the first time, I wished I had as quick a brain as Henry.

"I did manage to save this," I said, holding up the Transylvanian glass bottle I'd retrieved from my pocket.

"Thanks, Dolf," said Henry, "but that manuscript was priceless," he added through gritted teeth. "Not to mention the information it could have given us about Dracula and the Snagov Beast."

I wasn't surprised that Henry was more concerned about losing a few bits of paper than the danger we had encountered. I looked up at the window. There was no further sign of our attackers. "How did you know the window was just above the ground?"

"I didn't," said Henry with a shrug. "It was just the only realistic way out." He glanced at the window. "It's the first time I've been glad I'm only twelve—we wouldn't have squeezed through otherwise!"

Doing my best to ignore the fact we might have fallen to our deaths, I asked the next big question. "What next?"

Henry had turned away and was looking out across the huddle of buildings between the sea and us.

"Now we go to Transylvania!" he said.

THE UNPRONOUNCEABLE PLACE

One of the best things about traveling with Henry Hunter is that he has access to the kind of resources that very few people have. After several calls and only a few hours later we took off from a private airfield at Denham in a Learjet registered to Hunter Electronics— heading to 'the land of vampires,' as Henry kept calling it. Once we were onboard he produced a small mountain of books about vampires that he began to speed-read, while I sank

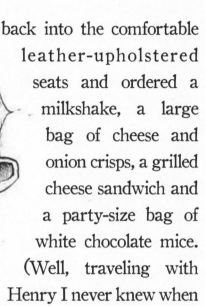

back into the comfortable leather-upholstered seats and ordered a milkshake, a large bag of cheese and onion crisps, a grilled cheese sandwich and a party-size bag of white chocolate mice. (Well, traveling with Henry I never knew when our next meal might be, and I have a tendency to get grumpy when I don't get enough to eat.)

I was rounding up the last few crumbs when Henry shoved a paper under my nose.

"Take a look at this, Dolf." I realized he'd reached the end of his book mountain and had moved on to an English newspaper. It was folded down to show a single small article.

ACADEMIC IN VAMPIRE ORDEAL

Respected historian Dr. Hans Trembling (55), currently residing in Whitby, suffered a terrifying ordeal when he was kidnapped from his home by two men speaking with foreign accents and taken to an unknown destination. There he was questioned at length about the history of Whitby's famous literary monster, Dracula. Having apparently failed to satisfy his captors, Dr. Trembling was placed in a coffin and the lid fastened down. He was only freed after his desperate cries attracted the attention of a local man (name withheld) who released him. Dr. Trembling is currently being treated for shock in Whitby General Hospital. The police are treating the incident as foul play and are continuing their investigations.

"So now we know," said Henry.

"Okay," I said, scanning the article again in case I'd missed anything "Um . . . what exactly do we know?"

"We know that there are some shady

people looking for the same things we are," Henry answered. "Probably the same ones we encountered in Whitby. We also know it all has something to do with Dracula." He beamed at me. "I think we haven't seen the last of those chaps in black."

That's the difference between Henry Hunter and me. He was positively looking forward to re-encountering the "shady people" whereas I would have been happy never to see them again.

It was only minutes later that we landed on a small airstrip at a place called Tigu Mures, which according to the in-flight information screen is pretty much bang slap in the middle of Romania.

We emerged from the warm interior of the jet into a blast of cold air and a steady curtain of rain that made a fog of the surrounding countryside. But at least the guide Henry had arranged was waiting for us with a comfortable air-conditioned car.

Mr. Radu Antonescu was a tall, dark-eyed man with a red-cheeked face. He had a large mustache that gave him a permanently dismal expression. But he spoke perfect English and seemed to have a good knowledge of the variety of sites to do with Dracula.

"There are many castles associated with the Count," he said through the driver's sliding screen as we drove away from the airstrip.

Henry nodded. "I know of half a dozen at least." He turned to me. "There's a lot of disagreement among the experts, Dolf. There are many who believe there actually was a Count Dracula, but they all have their own ideas about who he was."

"May I suggest," said Mr. Antonescu, "that we begin with Castle Bran? There are many strange stories surrounding that castle."

Henry squinted at Mr. Antonescu, as if he was trying to work something out, but then sat back and nodded. "Okay, Castle Bran it is," he said.

After this brief exchange we all fell silent—the only noise was the rustle of the peanut packet I'd found in the limo's minibar. As I munched I wondered just who the dark-clad people were who had attacked us in Whitby and stolen Jonathan Harker's manuscript. Mr. Antonescu said nothing more—though once or twice I caught him looking at us strangely in the rearview mirror. Still, Henry Hunter tends to get that kind of look all the time, so I paid little attention to it.

We drove for a couple of hours, our altitude climbing steadily. Henry appeared to fall

asleep, while I looked out of the window at the endless impenetrable forest we were tunneling through.

The next thing I knew, Henry was shaking me. "Wake up, Dolf, we're here."

"Where's 'here'?" I asked, trying to get rid of the dull feeling in my head.

Henry replied with something that sounded like Turkey Vest and which I later learned was actually Tirgoviste. I never did learn to pronounce it properly.

Mr. Antonescu had booked us a room in a hotel that he said was "very popular with the tourists." I had to assume that there weren't many tourists about, because we were the only guests.

After breakfast the next day (a cold porridge-like concoction that has to go down as one of the worst meals I've ever tasted—and on our adventures there have been some

very strange ones), we headed off along a series of switchback roads, heading north and seemingly always upwards. The rain of the previous day had thinned and a watery sunlight filled the landscape—though it did little to cheer it up. The scenery was certainly spectacular, if a bit grim. Mountains frequently overshadowed the road, rising on both sides into lowering cloud. Thick swatches of trees clustered everywhere, making the place seem even darker.

"Listen to this, Dolf," Henry said, looking up from the guide book he'd "borrowed" from the hotel. "It says here that it was only in the early twentieth century, some time after Bram Stoker's novel had appeared, that the outside world learned the real identity of Dracula. Until then it had been assumed he was just a story. Then a couple of scholars had visited Transylvania, along with the adjacent countries of Moldavia and Walachia, where they discovered that a fifteenth-century warrior called Vlad Tepes—that's pronounced 'Tep-esh,' Dolf— had earned the nickname 'the Impaler' because of his cheerful habit of impaling prisoners of war on sharp stakes."

"Nice," I interjected, thinking that medieval warriors clearly didn't like to mess around.

"Anyway, that much I already knew," Henry said. "But it also says here that he was part of a secret organization called 'The Order of the Dragon.' That's probably how he came to be called Dracula, because—did you know this, Dolf?—the word 'dracul' can mean either dragon or devil."

"So the old Count's name really means 'son of the dragon?'" I asked, trying to keep up.

"That's right! And get this, Dolf. When the old boy died, probably around 1476, he was buried in a great big tomb." He paused and closed the book with a snap. "Guess where, Dolf?

"Somewhere near here?" I guessed.

"Snagov," said Henry triumphantly.

The light bulb in my head flashed on at last. "The same place as the beast?"

"Yep, that's right, Dolf. And what's more, when they opened up the tomb about a hundred years after, it was empty!"

"So does that mean Dracula *is* the beast?"

"Well, he could be. But if you remember, the note we found suggested they were actually two separate things—that maybe Dracula became a vampire because of the Snagov Beast . . ."

"So what does that mean . . . ?" I said, leaving the sentence hanging.

"We have to go there, of course!" said Henry. "But as we're already on our way, let's see if the castles around here have anything to tell us first."

As we drove on, I stared out of the window at the wild countryside, easily understanding

how any writer would be inspired to set a novel about vampires, werewolves, or monsters here. Every few miles we passed the ruins of some old castle or monastery. Mr. Antonescu told us the area had been overrun by the Turks a number of times and these ruins were the result. He made it sound as though it had only just happened, but in fact most of it seemed to date back to the thirteenth and fourteenth centuries—the same period as Vlad Tepes.

"He is one of our greatest heroes, you know," volunteered Mr. Antonescu. "Despite the terrible things he did, he saved the country from being invaded."

We stopped for lunch in a small village called Cimpulung. We ate our bowls of meatball soup (infinitely better than the breakfast offering) in a little restaurant room

we had to ourselves at first, before a small, thin fellow with very sharp eyes sat down at the table opposite.

Mr. Antonescu put down his spoon and whispered, "If I'm not mistaken, that's Mathias Corvinus! He's known in the area for being a venerable expert on all matters to do with the history of Vlad Tepes."

Henry looked doubtful, but I nudged him regardless. "Should we talk to him? It could be a chance to find out more about what's going on here."

"Okay, I guess I can see no harm in it," Henry said, scraping the last of his soup. He tapped the skinny man on the shoulder and said something in Romanian, which I can only guess was Hello.

After a brief exchange, Mathias Corvinus

came and joined us at our table, while Mr. Antonescu went to fill up the car with gas.

"You are here," said the expert on Vlad the Impaler, "in search of the history of our great Count Tepes?"

I nodded, but Mr. Corvinus frowned. "You are aware of the foolish stories that are told about him. Most people who come here are looking for wampires."

I had to force myself to suppress a snort of laughter at his thick accent.

"We know about that," said Henry, "but we're really interested in the history of the country."

This was obviously the right thing to say because Mr. Corvinus lost some of his rather frosty demeanor and began to talk about various historical characters with unpronounceable names.

After a bit I stopped listening—until I heard Henry say something about reports of vampire activity. A long silence followed, punctuated by some throat clearing from Mr. Corvinus. Finally he said: "That is nonsense. No such things happen here!" All the frostiness was back, but Henry wasn't put off.

"I'm not saying there's any truth in it, but the reports remain. . . ."

"What reports?" demanded Mr. Corvinus. "I have heard nothing of any such things."

I remember thinking that if there were any such reports I hadn't heard them either. Then Henry caught my eye in a way I knew meant, "Play along with this, Dolf." He obviously wanted our "expert" to tell him something and this was clearly the quickest way to do it.

I thought on my feet. "Um, yes, um, the reports were pretty definite about signs of vampire activity in this area," I lied.

At this Mr. Corvinus suddenly gave in. All the stiffness went out of him and I suddenly saw that it wasn't that he was angry—he was frightened.

He stood up suddenly and walked across to the restaurant window. He looked out and then carefully drew the curtains. Then he came and sat down again and looked at Henry and me.

"I do not know how you hear of these things, Mr. Hunter, but it is true . . . there are stories. . . ." He hesitated. "If anyone at my university were to hear me repeating such things, I would be ridiculed."

"I promise that whatever you say won't go any further," said Henry firmly.

"It is the case that there have been as many as six or seven reports of strange, dark things lurking in the hills around the village. Several animals—including a cow—have been found drained of blood. You must understand," he went on, "it does not take very much to start people talking of vampires, in this of all places."

Henry was silent for a moment. I wondered if I should change the subject, or think of something intelligent to say. But then HH asked, "Have there been any other visitors around here, anyone out of the ordinary?"

Mr. Corvinus bit his lip. "There were some people here, just a few days ago. They were in a big black car and they spoke no Romanian. When they talked to the people in the village they seemed friendly enough, but I heard afterwards that they threatened some of those who live in more remote areas."

Henry leaned forward. "Do you happen to know what they were asking about?"

"Yes," said Mr. Corvinus. "The same thing as you. Any unusual things happening. Any strangers in the area. And . . . if they had seen any . . . young . . . for information. . . ."

I gasped at this revelation, but Henry seemed unaffected.

"Thank you," he said, smiling. "You've been very helpful, Mr. Corvinus."

Our guest cleared his throat several times and stood up to go.

At that moment the lights went out. The restaurant room, which was already dim because of the closed curtains, suddenly went very dark. And by that, I mean thick, impenetrable darkness that made me feel as if I had gone blind or as if someone had wrapped a thick scarf around my head. Frozen to the spot, I heard something—it sounded as if someone had tried to move and fallen over a chair or table, while someone else shouted something in Romanian. But it was another noise that got my attention—a curious scratching, as if something with very long claws was moving about—right there in the room!

Then, and I know this is going to be hard to believe, I was lifted up. . . . Yep, straight off the ground.

It felt as if something—or someone—with cold, hard hands, literally yanked me off my feet, spun me over so that I was lying horizontally, and then suspended me midair.

At the same time, the room became ice cold.

Castle Dracula—Maybe

When you can't see, your other senses get really sharp.

I heard a cork being pulled from a bottle. Then the sound of liquid being splashed about. A harsh cry followed and suddenly I was falling.

I hit the ground hard, winded and seeing stars. Then, just as suddenly as they had gone out, the lights came back on.

The scene they revealed was surprisingly less chaotic than I expected. Mr. Corvinus was standing in the middle of the room, exactly where he had been when he got up to go. He hadn't moved. I don't think he could. His eyes were shut and both his arms were wrapped tightly around his narrow chest.

Henry was standing by the door, as calm as ever. In his hand was a familiar glass bottle.

As I sat up, gasping for air, Henry looked concerned.

"You okay, Dolf?"

I couldn't get any words out, so I just nodded. Then, as my lungs finally started working properly, I croaked, "What just happened?"

"I'm not sure," said Henry. "But I think we were visited by a vampire."

I had feared this, but hadn't dared think it until now. While I felt at my neck for bites, Henry picked up a stopper from the floor and stuck it back into the small bottle. He saw my enquiring look. "I thought it a good idea to put a little Holy Water in it. You never know when you might need it when you visit vampire country. . . ."

Henry was interrupted by a crash and we both looked round quickly—Mr. Corvinus had fallen over. His eyes were still tight shut and he was as stiff as a corpse. Henry went into action. He grabbed a glass of water from the table and dribbled a bit between the old chap's lips. As it trickled into his mouth and ran down his cheeks he started spluttering and slowly opened one eye.

"It's okay, Mr. Corvinus, it's gone— whatever it was."

Slowly, Mr. Corvinus sat up. "Are you sure?"

"Yep. All gone. Nothing to worry about at all."

Mr. Corvinus started shaking. "You should not have come here, Mr. Hunter," he said. "No good can come of it."

He got up to go and bowed politely to us both.

"I assume that you will be returning home

tomorrow?" he said, his voice lilting at the end with what was clearly hope.

"Good grief, no!" said Henry, his eyebrows raised in genuine surprise. "As soon as Mr. Antonescu comes back we're heading to Castle Bran."

And so, minutes later, we were driving further into the mountains. The road curved up steadily through fog until it finally emerged into thin sunlight. It was the first time since our arrival in the country that it had stopped raining and I for one was glad of it. The countryside, now I could see it, was impressive—full of deep gorges and steep mountainsides, mostly covered by a thick blanket of trees.

We arrived at the town of Bran after a couple of hours and drove up a steep incline to the castle. I felt as if we should have been in an old-fashioned coach drawn by black horses with nodding plumes, rather than a modern

car—but I have to say my imagination was already a bit overworked by then.

I'm not really into castles or history, but its smooth, white walls and towers topped by crimson roofs made the place stand out among the darker colors of the surrounding country. The gate was wide and had one of those iron portcullis things—as if it was built to keep out anything. Or to keep anything in, for that matter. I thought it looked a bit familiar and couldn't work out why until I realized it had been used as a location for several old horror movies. Somehow it didn't quite look the same without lens filters and artificial mist.

Henry was chattering away to Mr. Antonescu about the history of the place—apparently the present castle was built over an even older one dated from the thirteenth century. Count Vlad the Impaler used it as one of several places from which he could ride out for a bit of pillaging—and of course plenty of impaling.

Mr. Antonescu talked to one of the custodians and we got the VIP tour of the castle. I suppose I was expecting crumbling walls and dark, dank corners matted with spiderwebs, but in fact there was nothing like that. The place was impressive in a weird, historical kind of way—lots of old furniture, even older-looking tapestries on the walls and wooden floorboards that creaked with every step. But it didn't really have much atmosphere—at least nothing like you'd expect of a place associated with the world's most famous vampire.

We finally arrived in the great hall—a huge, echoing room with a vast stone fireplace and several moth-eaten tapestries hanging on the walls. Over the mantelpiece hung a portrait of a dark-haired, unsmiling man wearing a funny kind of hat (well, I thought it was funny, anyway). Our guide paused in front of it and announced in a very deep and serious voice, "And here, of course, we have the portrait of the notorious Count Dracula!"

I was disappointed. I couldn't see any fangs and he wasn't wearing a cloak, but then nothing seemed to be quite what I expected.

Henry looked up at the portrait and said, "Actually, that's not the Count all."

The custodian came over all huffy and reddened.

"I can assure you this is indeed the famous Dracula!"

"Sorry, but it's not," answered Henry with one of his warmest smiles. "Whoever this is, it's not him. The painting is at least a hundred years too modern, the costume is wrong and anyway, Vlad Tepes didn't look like that at all."

Hearing raised voices, a couple of tourists drifted over in our direction, staring curiously. The custodian opened and closed his mouth a few times, while Henry pulled out one of the large books he had been consulting in the car and opened it at a page that showed a similar portrait to the one on the wall, except that the dark-faced man in the book was a lot more sinister and strange. There was something about the face that gave me goosebumps, even in broad daylight.

Suddenly the castle seemed a lot colder and weirder. Our guide stood there twisting his hands and looking uncomfortable, while Mr. Antonescu looked at the floor.

"Never mind," said Henry brightly, as if

suddenly realizing he'd upset everyone. "This castle is a really great place and it's been fantastic visiting it." He pulled me and Mr. Antonescu away from the custodian, who seemed relieved to answer the questions of a group of elderly tourists.

Henry turned to Mr. Antonescu. "Do you think we can go to the real Castle Dracula now?"

"But this is—"

"Sorry," interrupted Henry. "What I mean is that I know this is one of his castles— it's just not the one I'm looking for."

Maybe it was my imagination, but I thought Mr. Antonescu looked a bit shifty. He drew himself up and stuck out his chin and said, "May I ask which castle it is you wish to see?"

"I was thinking of the Red Tower," answered Henry, beaming at our guide as if he had just offered him a Mars bar.

Mr. Antonescu definitely turned pale.

"But there is nothing to see there," he said. "Only a broken ruin. And it is so difficult to get to. . . ."

"I'm sure we can find it with your help," said Henry firmly.

I knew that look and tone of voice. Once HH makes up his mind you might as well just give in and go along with him, because there's no way he's going to change it.

Mr. Antonescu huffed and puffed a bit, but in the end he gave in.

I wanted to ask Henry why we were at Castle Bran at all if it was the Red Castle he'd wanted to visit all along. But before I could get him alone to pose my question it dawned on me that perhaps my friend had been simply humoring our guide's first suggestion—Henry knew how best to play adults, especially when he needed to engineer his own way.

As we left the castle I had a sudden feeling that I was being watched. You know that creepy feeling you get sometimes when something is not quite right but you can't say why? Anyway, I looked back and thought I saw a figure standing in the shadows of the gatehouse. I blinked and it seemed to vanish as if it had never been there. I opened my mouth to tell Henry what I thought I'd seen, and then decided not to. He'd only tell me for the umpteenth time that I had an overactive imagination.

We got back into the car and left Castle Bran in silence. As the road wound even further up into the mountains I was dying to ask Henry what he knew about the Red Castle, but I had to wait until we stopped for fuel at a roadside gas station. While Mr. Antonescu was chatting to the pump attendant I got my chance.

Henry shrugged. "Castle Bran is the most famous—the one all the tourists go to. My research tells me it has nothing to do with the real mystery. But you know what I always say,

Dolf. Leave no stone unturned. It was worth going if only to eliminate it." He hesitated for a moment, then added in a low voice, "Besides, I wanted to see if we'd be followed."

"Followed!" I said, then realized I'd spoken loudly. "Followed?" I whispered. "And were we?"

"Oh yes," said Henry quietly. "There's been the same black car on our tail since we left Tirgoviste. . . . But don't look now, Dolf. I'd rather wait and see what they do next."

It was a struggle not to look back down the road we had just driven up. I stared over at Mr. Antonescu. I wondered if he knew we were being followed, and if this accounted for his nervous behavior.

"Don't worry, Dolf," said Henry breezily. "The fact that we are being followed means we're getting closer to solving the mystery. All I want to do now is get to the real castle— or at least what I think is the real one."

"This 'Red Tower' you mentioned?"

"Yes. It's much older than Castle Bran and all the experts say it's where Vlad Tepes spent most of his time. If there's anything to find out I think it'll be there. I was humoring Mr. Antonescu when he suggested going to Bran first. No harm in getting him on our side. And there's something else, Dolf. Guess what else is just a few miles away?

My brain went into overdrive. "Um . . . Snagov?" I guessed.

"Got it in one!"

I tried to push down the bad feeling in my gut. The adventurous side of me wanted to track down a beast. I just happened to have a more fearful side too, which I was right then finding hard to ignore. "Mr. Antonescu doesn't seem like he wants to go there."

Henry frowned. "No. He doesn't. I can't decide whether he knows something we don't, or is just afraid. I suppose we'll find out sooner or later."

At that moment Mr. Antonescu rejoined us. He seemed unaccountably more cheerful as we drove on, though he still found time to point out that the way up to the Red Tower— or Castle Arges as I learned was its real name—was arduous.

"We will stay in a place I have found for you tonight. Then, in the morning—if you still wish to proceed—we will make our way to the castle."

"If it's all the same to you, Mr. Antonescu, I'd rather go up there tonight," Henry said.

I glanced at the rearview mirror. Mr. Antonescu looked as if he'd been hit in the face. I grabbed the door handle as he swerved the car over to the side of the road and turned around to glare at us.

"Mr. Hunter," he said, "I am instructed to take you wherever you wish to go. But it is also my duty to keep you safe. The Red Castle is not a good place. It has a bad reputation and the way up to it is difficult, especially in the dark. Surely you do not wish to go there now?"

"That's exactly what I do want, Mr. Antonescu," answered Henry firmly. He lowered his voice. "I'm sure you know we've been followed ever since we arrived in your country. Then there's that business back in Tirgoviste. What exactly was it that paid us a visit? I think we'll only get to the bottom of this mystery by going to the place with the bad rep after dark."

While Mr. Antonescu sat there with his eyes bulging, Henry went on. "If you don't want to come along that's up to you. Just take us as near to the castle as you can. I'm sure we'll be just fine on our own, won't we, Dolf?"

I wasn't at all sure we'd be "just fine," but I already knew that being around Henry Hunter meant never expecting an easy ride. So I grinned as hard as I could and nodded as if we regularly visited castles home to vampires at night.

Mr. Antonescu stared at us for a bit longer. Then he shrugged. "Very well. If you are so foolish as to risk your lives, I cannot prevent it."

He accelerated away, just a little bit faster than I liked on those narrow roads, but that wasn't the thing really bothering me. Nor was I thinking about our impending visit to Castle Arges. No, my brain was still focused on the fact that someone—or something— had been following us ever since we entered the country.

The question was, who was watching us, and why?

THE RED TOWER

The Red Tower, aka Castle Arges or Castle Dracula, stands at the top of a mountain. While I scavenged the minibar for any remaining edible snacks (I found an out-of-date cereal bar and a packet of ginger nut cookies), assuming dinner would be the last thing on Henry's mind, Mr. Antonescu took us about halfway up—as far as he said the road was navigable. Then he pointed to where a narrow track snaked off amid the trees. A very worn and battered sign inscribed with the name of the castle in Romanian was

nailed to the trunk of a big tree. Someone had scrawled other words across it: **NU SE POATE**. I had guessed what they meant even before Henry told me: *Keep Out*.

It was clear Mr. Antonescu thought we were completely mad, and to be honest I wasn't entirely convinced we weren't. But this was life with Henry Hunter, and even then, I wouldn't have swapped it for anything. He stood there while Henry produced two large flashlights from the boot of the car, along with two well-stuffed backpacks, one of which he handed to me.

"Should be everything we need for tonight, Dolf," he said, grinning. I took the rucksack and tried to return the smile. Then I turned to Mr. Antonescu, who looked a rather forlorn figure standing by the car. He watched us with a look that clearly said he did not expect to ever see us again.

Henry set a cracking pace and for the next

hour neither of us had much breath for talking. The way was steep and the path soon petered out, replaced by rough scree that had us slipping and sliding and falling over several times.

"Not far now, Dolf," Henry said every so often, as if he'd climbed this mountain hundreds of times before. And finally, it wasn't. We emerged from a grove of trees onto the mountain peak. And there in front of us in the gathering dark was the real Castle Dracula.

Unlike Castle Bran it was small, and looked a lot older—and somehow nastier. A narrow wooden bridge spanned a very deep gorge between us and the gates, which hung off their hinges as if they'd been blown out by some kind of explosion.

In the darkness, big shadows hung everywhere around us like bat wings, and far below we could see the lights of a couple of villages glowing dimly. There was just enough light from the moon to get

a glimpse of huge mountain peaks to the north. Then clouds drew across the moon and darkness rushed in on us like a cloak.

"No going back now, Dolf," said Henry, in a chirpy voice—he said this because he was happy about it, not because he thought I needed reminding. He was right, of course. There was no way we could find our way back down the mountain in the utter darkness. This was what adventure was to Henry Hunter—all about the unknown and the dangerous. And this was one of our most dangerous situations yet.

Henry switched on his flashlight, which was a powerful LED one that was as bright as a searchlight. Shadows jumped about everywhere, and for a moment I thought I saw something solid moving by the castle wall— maybe a flash of eyes—but just as quickly it was gone. "Did you see that?" I asked.

"What?" said Henry, swinging the flashlight around.

"I thought I saw something moving."

"Probably just a wolf," said Henry.

"There are wolves around here?" I said, wondering why I hadn't guessed this before. But Henry wasn't listening. He was shining the flashlight into the gateway of the castle.

"Let's go, Dolf," he said, and set off across the wooden bridge.

Without a better suggestion, I followed, the bridge boards creaking ominously every time either of us put a foot on them. I couldn't help but imagine the bridge collapsing, sending us plummeting to our grisly deaths in the valley below. I was too young to die.

But my worries were unfounded, and we soon found ourselves up close and personal with the castle wall.

It was a lot more ruined than I had realized. Big cracks split the walls and in places there were just heaps of rubble. But the gatehouse still looked pretty solid despite the broken gates, and with our flashlights held out in front of us we passed under the frowning stones and emerged into the courtyard.

By daylight it must have been impressive—at night it was just plain scary. Although I didn't actually ask Henry, I was sure that at moment even he would agree. Dark shadows lay in wait everywhere, and when we shone our flashlights into them they seemed to swallow the light and turn it into something feeble. We could just make out the shape of the castle: a rough octagon with towers at each corner. Most of them were ruined, with big gaping holes that looked a lot like eyes watching us.

A thick carpet of leaves rustled underfoot—if there was something here waiting for us,

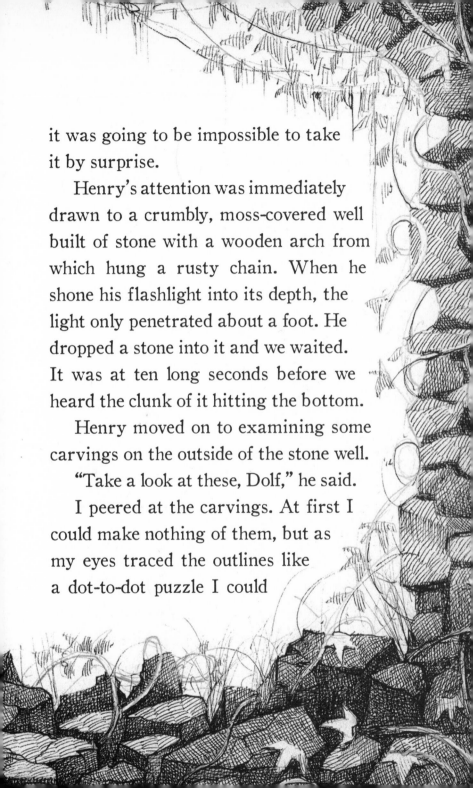

it was going to be impossible to take
it by surprise.

Henry's attention was immediately
drawn to a crumbly, moss-covered well
built of stone with a wooden arch from
which hung a rusty chain. When he
shone his flashlight into its depth, the
light only penetrated about a foot. He
dropped a stone into it and we waited.
It was at ten long seconds before we
heard the clunk of it hitting the bottom.

Henry moved on to examining some
carvings on the outside of the stone well.

"Take a look at these, Dolf," he said.

I peered at the carvings. At first I
could make nothing of them, but as
my eyes traced the outlines like
a dot-to-dot puzzle I could

make out a row of sharp stakes embedded in the earth, each one decorated by a skull.

"Fascinating," said Henry. But as I stared harder at the carvings, Henry's attention had been taken by something else. He was shining his flashlight on the ground a few feet to the left of the well. There, half hidden by the leaves, was a big iron ring.

"There's supposed to be an underground chamber somewhere here," said Henry, setting off across the courtyard towards the iron ring.

He never got to it.

Three steps away, the ground gave way and Henry vanished with a yell that echoed around the great stone walls. It was followed by silence.

If you've ever wondered what the phrase "rooted to the spot" means, this described me right then. Every muscle in my body simply stopped working for at least a minute. I tried to call out but all I could manage was a croak.

Come on, Dolf! I told myself, and took a couple of deep breaths. That made me feel better. I shone my flashlight at the spot where Henry had vanished and saw a large hole framed by some splintered wooden planks. Slowly, one step at a time, testing the ground before I put any weight on it, I crept nearer to the edge of the hole. Finally I was able to peer down.

Darkness. I guessed that however far Henry had fallen, his flashlight must have gone out. A strange musty smell came from the hole. I shouted as loudly as I could, "Henry! Are you okay?"

Silence.

I leaned over the hole and shouted again. Still no answer. Then, just as I was beginning to give up, a faint sound drifted towards me from the depth. The sound of someone struggling. Then, distant but clear, and very echoey, came a voice. Henry Hunter's voice.

"I'm okay, Dolf." A wave of relief flooded through me. As I stared down, a very dim light appeared. A match. Of course—Henry always had a box of matches on him.

"Can you climb out?" I yelled.

"I can't see any way to do that, Dolf," came Henry's voice. "I think I'm going to need a hand."

"Um, did you pack a rope? I called down.

"Only one—but it's in my pack," he answered. "Which is down here with me."

"Okay," I said, trying to think quickly about what else I could use as a rope. "I'll see if I can find something up here."

"Just where do you think you're going to find rope around here?" said a voice behind me.

I jumped, my heart beating wildly. I spun round and shone my flashlight into the darkness. At first all I could see was a shadowy silhouette.

My first thought was: *I don't think it's big enough to be a monster*.

My second was: *Who says vampires have to*

be huge?

And my third was: *it's a girl's voice.*

"Could you point that thing somewhere else?" she said. Her voice was clear and low and she spoke English with only a trace of an accent. I lowered the flashlight obediently, but its peripheral glow still allowed me to get a proper look at her. I guessed she was around fourteen or fifteen. She would have been pretty if she weren't scowling. Her dark hair was cut short and stuck up in spikes and she was clad from head to foot in black leather. But it was her eyes that got my attention.

They were bright blue, and in the reflected flashlight they seemed almost to glow. (I know that sounds lame, but if you'd been there you would have said the same.)

I had a sudden, powerful desire to apologize. For being there. For shining a light on her. For existing. Finally I managed to get some words out, "My friend. He's down there. Can you help us?"

"It's amazing you've survived this long," she said. She leaned forward with her hands on her hips, and peered down into the hole. "You down there. Where are you exactly?"

If Henry was surprised to hear a girl's voice he didn't sound it. "I'm in a kind of chamber. About ten yards down, I think."

"Can you see a stone that's a different color from the rest? Just above your head?"

"Hang on a minute," Henry's voice echoed. Down in the darkness I saw another match flare briefly.

"I see it," Henry called, still sounding very

calm despite the situation.

"Good. Press it," ordered the girl.

I heard the sound of stone scraping against stone, which went on for a minute then stopped.

"It's a hidden door," Henry said, quite matter-of-factly. But then he was used to this kind of adventure—nothing much shocked Henry Hunter. "And . . . a passageway."

"Follow it," the girl told him. "It will bring you out onto the side of the mountain. We'll meet you there."

"Okay," said Henry. "See you in a bit." Then he added, "Everything all right up there, Dolf?"

"Um . . . I think so!" I called back.

"He thinks so," muttered the girl. "How like a boy."

"See you soon, Henry," I called into the darkness, but there was no answer. Henry had already gone.

Bella

I followed the girl as best I could, though she moved with surprising speed—despite never seeming to break into a run—and I was hampered by my backpack. I felt glad that the moon, almost full, had appeared from behind the cover of clouds. By its light I could see well enough to avoid falling over.

In what seemed no more than a few minutes we arrived at a place where a couple of hardy trees grew out of the mountain. The girl slowed to a stop, reached out and pulled aside a curtain of branches, revealing a dark hole leading into the mountain. I wondered if we were going in, but then I heard the scuffle of footsteps, and Henry emerged.

Unusually for HH, he looked a bit the worse for wear. He had cobwebs and leaves in his hair, his jacket was torn at the shoulder and I spotted a cut on the side of his face that oozed a trickle of blood.

"That was impressive," Henry said, beaming. "How did you know the passage was there?"

The girl narrowed her eyes as if she didn't particularly like what she saw. "I live around here, silly boy," she said simply.

"Well, thanks anyway." Henry stuck out a hand. "My name's Henry by the way, and this is Dolf."

"Bella," snapped the girl, ignoring Henry's hand. "You shouldn't be in this place after dark. It's not safe."

"You mean, because of the vampires?" said Henry, his voice steady.

The girl hesitated before she answered, and I thought I saw a gleam of laughter in her eyes. "Many different kinds of creatures live in these mountains," she said, avoiding the question. "It is not wise to be out here."

"You don't seem to mind," said Henry.

I glanced between the two of them, not sure where this conversation was going.

The girl frowned. "That's because I know the place and the place knows me. My family has lived around here for a long time."

"Well, in that case, do you have any idea what these mean?" Henry pulled a crumpled piece of paper from his pocket. As he passed it over I caught a glimpse of some roughly sketched drawings. They depicted people with either spears or swords attacking a huge wormlike creature with a long spiked tail that spat fire.

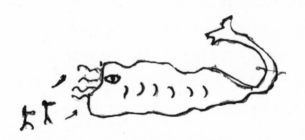

The girl's reaction was instant. Her face clouded with anger and she rattled off a whole series of sentences in what I assumed was Romanian. Then, not knowing Henry was actually pretty fluent, she seemed to realize who we were and switched to English.

"Where did you find those?" she demanded, staring so hard at Henry that I thought he might actually burst into flames.

Of course HH wasn't fazed. "They were scratched onto the walls of the well shaft," he said. "While I was down there I copied them. I thought they might be useful."

"Useful for what?" said the girl.

"It's a long story," answered Henry.

The girl folded her arms and continued her stare. In the moonlight her eyes seemed to glow again. "So tell me," she said.

I could see Henry weighing up whether or not to be truthful. I have to admit I was quite surprised when he told her how our adventure began, with the *Unbelievable Times* article. Henry sketched our adventures briefly, and when he mentioned the name Whitby the girl's eyes flickered—she clearly recognized it, but said nothing. But I noticed he did not mention the mysterious attackers in Whitby, or the strange events at the restaurant yesterday.

When he finished, the girl stared at him in silence for a moment. Then she looked away, up towards the castle and then at the moon, which was lower in the sky now.

"It will be dawn soon. I must go home." She looked at both of us intently and said, "You should not be here. It is not safe. Go back where you came from."

"I'm afraid we can't do that—not till we find out what's going on." Henry fixed his eyes on her. "Why have you been following us?"

Good old Henry. Only HH could get away with being so direct.

At first I thought the girl wasn't going to answer. Then she suddenly laughed, a surprisingly pleasant sound in the darkness.

Just as quickly, she went back to frowning again.

"I was curious. Two English boys, wandering about my country, asking questions about vampires. Coming up here, after dark, alone. You are either very stupid or very brave—I cannot decide which."

Henry flashed his famous grin, and pushed his hair back from his brows. "So what can you tell us about the pictures at the bottom of the well?" he asked.

"Not now," replied the girl. "It is better for us all if we leave this place." She seemed a bit uneasy and kept glancing at the sky as if looking for something.

"I will guide you down the mountain to the road," she continued. "I hope your man with the car will return for you at dawn."

"Perhaps we can talk later?" Henry persisted.

"Perhaps," the girl responded, glancing at the sky again.

Maybe because we were going downhill or perhaps because the girl knew the way better than us, we were soon standing by the roadside. There was no sign of Mr. Antonescu. I wasn't surprised. I glanced at my watch—it was almost four a.m. Suddenly I felt tired. We had been on the mountain for most of the night and at that moment the idea of a shower, a hot chocolate, and a warm bed seemed more important than solving any mystery.

"Take my advice. Go away from this place," the girl said to us again.

Then she was gone, so suddenly that neither of us could see where or how she went.

"Well, she wasn't very friendly," I said.

"I'm pretty sure she doesn't get out much," answered Henry thoughtfully. "Did you notice the strange dialect of Romanian she spoke when she got angry? Really old fashioned. A bit like if you or I spoke medieval English."

I was still thinking that a) I had no idea what dialect the girl spoke, and b) how weird it would be if HH and I started spouting some old language, especially as I was pretty terrible at anything other than basic English, when there was a sudden rush of footsteps. Before we could react, about a dozen dark figures surrounded us. I tried to stay calm even as I noticed they all had nunchukus in their hands and one carried what looked like a rather big knife.

Not this lot again, I thought, steeling myself for a repeat of the punching and kicking we'd received in Whitby.

But to my surprise we were spared, because a brilliant light suddenly illuminated the scene, accompanied by a noise loud enough to wake any undead vampires who might have been hanging around. I had just time to see that the girl who'd just left us was straddling a large black motorbike before all hell broke loose.

The bike skidded to a stop and the girl leaped gracefully from the saddle, leaving the engine running. She hit the group of startled attackers like a sledgehammer, scattering them in all directions. Cries. Yells. Screams. Henry and I just stood there staring as the slender girl cut into the gang like a knife into a block of cheese.

It was then that both they and we spotted the girl's fine set of fangs, and eyes that blazed with light.

In the heat of the realization, I couldn't help but shout out, "She's a vampire!"

Our attackers who were still standing saw Bella's face clearly in the light from her motorbike, and they reacted exactly as you'd expect. More cries. More screams. More yells. I distinctly heard one man shout, "The Count's daughter is among us!" Then they fled, with those who could racing away, and those who'd received Bella's punches and kicks limping or staggering off into the darkness.

As quickly as it began the attack was over. Bella returned to her bike, hauled it on to its stand and switched off the engine. The night was suddenly very quiet, though I could almost hear Henry's mind ticking over as he struggled to decide what to ask about first.

In the end he settled on a rather shaky, "Thank you. That's twice you've saved us."

Bella shrugged. "I told you to go home," she said. The fangs had vanished—withdrawn, just like in the movies—and her eyes were clear blue again. I found this comforting since I assumed it meant we were not about to be attacked, but at the same time I saw again the small trickle of blood on Henry's face.

Bella must have caught me looking, because she began to laugh. "Don't worry," she said. "I won't attack you. I gave all that up two hundred years ago."

Henry and I both chuckled—a bit hysterically—while Bella leaned against her bike and studied us seriously.

"Who exactly are you?" Henry managed at last.

"Bella Dracul," she answered without hesitation. "The only daughter of Prince Vlad Dracula."

I gaped, trying to take this in. I had no doubt she was telling the truth. Meanwhile Henry's logical mind kicked in.

"I thought vampires couldn't have children."

"My father was not always a vampire," returned Bella.

"But . . ." I just about found my voice as questions still ran around my head.

"It is a mistake everyone makes. Tourists! Film people! What do they know? Always coming here in search of *clues*."

"You mean there was another vampire before Dracula?" I asked.

"Of course. Many more. All of them are gone now. Or else are in hiding, like me."

Henry was surprisingly quiet, but I had been doing the math. "If you're Vlad Dracul's daughter you must be . . . over five hundred years old!"

Bella tossed her head. "Don't you know it's rude to ask a girl her age?" she said with a smile, then her eyes turned serious. "I was born in 1461, not far from here. My mother was a mortal, like my father at that time. It was only later that he . . ." She paused, as if she didn't want to say the words.

"You mean that your father . . . made you a vampire?" said Henry, breaking the silence.

Bella gave a quick nod, and I thought I detected something like sadness on her pale face. She looked up at the sky again. The first edge of greenish light was creeping above the mountains. "I must be gone from here. It will be dawn soon and that at least is one story that's true—my kind cannot be out in sunlight. But don't worry, I do not think those people will be back in a hurry. I will come to you tomorrow night and we will talk some more."

And with that the girl who was Dracula's daughter climbed back onto her bike, started the engine and roared off into the night.

More About The Beast

Henry and I didn't talk much after Bella left us to wait for Mr. Antonescu. We were both exhausted and I could see that HH was digesting the information we had gathered that night.

"Who do you think they are—that lot in black?" I ventured at one point.

"No idea. But I'll tell you one thing—they knew who Bella was. The real question is, Dolf, not who they are but what they want with us."

I frowned at Henry, wondering if that fall

down the well had affected his brain. "Um, well, I'm guessing they aren't exactly friendly, since they keep attacking us."

"Perhaps," mused Henry. "But that was before they knew we were friends with Bella Dracul."

"Friends," I repeated. I supposed we were. But the idea was so enormous—that we were actually friends with Dracula's daughter— that it silenced me. Then again, were we really? Friends, I mean? Actual friends? Or was there another reason why Bella had helped us?

Mr. Antonescu returned for us an hour after Bella had left. He looked surprised to find us still alive, but although I could tell he really wanted to ask about our night, he drove in silence. We were soon checking in to another of those tourist-friendly hotels he seemed to like. Henry and I fell into our beds with barely a word spoken.

When I woke, the sun was already low in the sky—I'd slept for most of the day. As usual Henry was up before me. I found him in the dining room working his way though a plate of eggs and bacon. I was starving, I realized, and ordered a double English breakfast with extra sausages. There was no sign of Mr. Antonescu—Henry told me he had gone off to put some more gas in the car.

"He's really bursting to know what happened," said Henry. "But of course we mustn't tell him. It's Bella's secret."

What I was more concerned about was how we were going to talk to Bella again without Mr. Antonescu finding out.

I needn't have worried.

We heard the rumble of the car as our guide returned from his trip, but he went off to bed without even looking in on us. About five minutes after the sun had set, as Henry and I were sitting in our room, we became aware that we were not alone. One minute we were poring over Henry's strange drawings from the well, and the next Bella was sitting in a chair next to us, looking at us with those strange intense eyes. Neither of us had any idea how she got in, though I was busy imagining coils of mist seeping under the door, as I'd seen in all the best Dracula movies.

"Still here then?" she said.

"Afraid so," answered Henry. "We're hoping you can give us a heads-up on some of this mystery. It's the best way to get rid of us," he added, grinning.

"Then I suppose I have no choice," said Bella, with a straight face but a glint of laughter in her eyes. "But first I want to know exactly what's happened to you—ever since you decided to follow that mention of vampires in the newspaper," she demanded.

"It's a long story," said Henry.

Bella folded her arms.

"I have all night," she said.

So Henry (with occasional additions from yours truly) told her the whole story this time, right from the moment he had read the article in the *Unbelievable Times* to the previous night's escapades. Bella listened closely until Henry finished his account. Then she sat back in her chair and crossed her leather-clad legs.

"So who do you think these people are—the ones who keep making your lives so difficult?" she asked.

"I was hoping you could tell us," said Henry.

"I have no idea," said Bella. She frowned. "They must know what you're doing here because they knew about the manuscript and where to find it. And they must have been following you, because they found you last night."

"I thought it was you who was following us," I put in.

Her blue eyes looked right through me. "Only for the last few days. I heard about two English schoolboys asking funny questions and thought I'd better check you silly boys out."

"So it was you at Cimpulung," said Henry. "Our invisible visitor!" He frowned. "Sorry about the Holy Water."

Bella shrugged in reply, and smiled, which made her face a lot nicer; then she seemed to realize what she was doing and stopped.

"It only stings a little," she said. "I wanted to scare you off."

"Why?" asked Henry.

"Far too many people come around here, poking about, thinking they can prove vampires exist—or that they don't. Tourists. Film people. Always wanting to know about the "evil" count Dracula. Sometimes I like to give them something to really think about."

"I promise we aren't trying to prove anything," said Henry. "All I want to do is find out the truth about the Snagov Beast."

Bella's face changed at once. Her eyes widened—as if she was both angry and even a bit afraid.

"You want nothing to do with that," she said sharply.

"So you've heard of it?" Henry said calmly.

Bella closed her eyes briefly, and then replied. "There have been rumors for many hundreds of years about something terrifying living in the mountains. My father mentioned it once, but even he seemed afraid. He warned me never to go anywhere near Snagov."

"But isn't that where your father's . . . um . . . grave is?" I blurted.

"Yes," Bella said bluntly. "But I do not go there, and I have already told you not to either."

Henry was looking thoughtful. "It could be the best way to get some answers."

Bella glared at both of us. "Listen to me," she said. "You are both just silly boys. In this country we take vampires seriously—for you it is just an adventure! My advice is that you go home as soon as you can and forget all about this place and what you have seen. In any case, I no longer want to talk about this."

Before either of us could say another word, she simply melted away into a drift of greenish smoke.

Henry stared at the spot where Bella had been.

"What now?" I asked, expecting Henry to say that we had to go to Snagov right away. Instead, he looked at me with an uncharacteristically mournful expression.

Then came the words I never expected to hear from the mouth of Henry Hunter. "Maybe she's right. Maybe we should just go home."

I was just too amazed to answer. Henry glanced at the window, where the moon peeked out from behind a passing cloud. He

sighed—something else he didn't usually do.

"Let's sleep on it, Dolf. No need to decide now."

I didn't sleep very well, I have to say. Maybe it was because I wasn't used to going to bed in the middle of the night and waking in the afternoon. When I did sleep, I dreamed about leather-clad vampires on motorbikes and strange beasts with big teeth and large claws.

Just after three p.m. I decided to get up, but when I looked for Henry I saw his bed was smooth and had clearly not been slept in.

Somewhat naively perhaps, I thought he'd probably gone for a walk, so I got up and washed in the tiny sink in the corner of the room. The water was cold and looked a bit rusty. All the time I was brushing my teeth I expected Henry to come bounding in with some piece of news or something else he'd discovered, but even after I had found my way to the dining area and chomped my way through some rather stale bread and cold sausage (I was starving yet again), there was still no sign of him.

Must be a long walk, I thought. I went outside—our car was still parked where we had left it the day before. There was no sign of Mr. Antonescu.

The area we were staying in was not particularly interesting by way of scenery—unless you like a lot of trees and hills and small red-roofed houses. I sat down on a bench outside the hotel door and watched the world go by. A man with a dog walked past, glancing at me sideways as he went.

Slowly, the sun sank down behind the mountains in a blaze of assorted colors and I began to worry. Not that I wasn't used to Henry vanishing for hours at a time, but given the present circumstances I couldn't help wondering just where he had gone and how long ago. I started to think I should do something. I just wasn't sure what.

Finally I got up, deciding to go in search of Mr. Antonescu. I knocked on the door to his room but there was no answer, so I went downstairs to find the hotel's owner. When I asked him if he'd seen Henry or our guide he simply shrugged and spouted a stream of Romanian.

Where had Henry gone?

I went back to our room and it was then that I found Henry's backpack missing, along with his flashlight. I was getting seriously worried, so I sat down on my bed and thought hard. One of two things must have happened. Either Henry had decided to go off on his own—I suspected in search of the Snagov Beast (by no means beyond him if he got really excited about something and couldn't wait for me to wake), or he had been taken by the mysterious people who had attacked us. Whichever was true, it meant Henry was in danger, and where was I, his trusty companion? Twiddling my thumbs in a place whose name I didn't know and almost certainly couldn't pronounce.

I stood up and reached for my own pack and flashlight. There was only one thing to do, only one person who could help—if she would. I had to find Dracula's daughter.

Hunting for Henry

The problem with going on adventures with someone who does most of the thinking is that when you get stranded in a tricky situation, it's not so easy to start doing all the thinking for yourself again.

But, as I began the long walk towards Castle Arges—the only place I knew of where I might find Bella—I tried anyway.

I realized that it was unlikely he'd gone on the next part of the quest on his own. First—and I wasn't being big-headed, but—Henry generally liked to have me around, and second, if he had left for Snagov, how had he planned to get there without Mr. Antonescu and the car?

This raised another question: where was Mr. Antonescu anyway? Had he simply got fed up with Henry's refusal to take his warnings, resigned from his job as our guide and gone home? Or, as I increasingly feared had happened to Henry, had he been taken by our attackers as well? Perhaps they were both lying dead—somewhere on the mountain? Had I failed Henry while I was sleeping? The thought sent trickles of terror down my spine.

So, here I was in search for Bella Dracul.

Now, don't get me wrong, I have nothing against vampires, especially when they're as good-looking as she was, but I couldn't help thinking about the whole blood-drinking thing. We only had her word for it that she had given up on all that kind of stuff two hundred years ago. After all, vampires need blood to survive, don't they? If we were really

friends, no problem, but I wasn't sure of that yet. What if she got a bit peckish and I ended up as a snack?

But all I could do was go with my best instinct, which was that I needed Bella if I had any chance of rescuing Henry alive. Luckily I didn't have to go far to find her— or rather, she found me. I was still a mile or so away from where we'd been attacked two nights ago when the night was split yet again by brilliant headlights. With a familiar roar the big black motorbike came hurtling out of the darkness and skidded to a stop right in front of me, throwing up a shower of sharp grit against my legs.

I stood there, nervously rubbing my shins, as Dracula's daughter turned off the engine and shot me a far-from-pleased-to-see-you stare.

"I thought I told you to go home," she said, looking past my shoulder for Henry. "Where's your friend?"

I began to feel uncomfortable, as if Henry's disappearance was somehow all my fault.

"I think he's been taken by someone!" I blurted out.

Bella put her head to one side. "No surprise there. Who took him?"

"That's the problem. I don't know. I woke up a couple of hours ago and he was gone. Bed not slept in, no sign of his backpack."

Bella frowned. "Did he leave a note?"

"No." I hesitated, then admitted, "I thought maybe he'd decided to go off after this beast thing on his own."

Bella cursed in Romanian (it needed no translation).

"Young and foolish!" she snapped. I wished I could have a bit of the softer Bella back, the Bella who seemed to want to befriend us. Then she stared hard at me. "And what are you doing here?"

"Um, I was . . . er . . . looking for you."

"I suppose you want me to help find your friend?"

"Well, there really isn't anyone else I can ask," I said sheepishly.

Bella looked up at the moon as it emerged from a mesh of dark clouds. The wind blew mournfully through the pines as I heard a creature howl somewhere in their depths. Turning back, Bella regarded me from head to toe.

Then she let out a small sigh and said: "It looks like I have no choice—if only to stop that silly boy from bringing down the sky on our heads!"

A few minutes later I found myself sitting behind Bella on her motorcycle, my arms around her waist and my face pressed into the soft leather of her shoulder, as she roared through the night.

Bella said that first she needed to go home to

consult some old records left by her father. I kept telling myself that there was really nothing strange about riding a motorbike with a seven-hundred-year-old vampire girl who seemed to think traveling at eighty miles an hour on narrow mountain roads was perfectly normal, and that we were only going to her home (the word 'lair' kept popping into my head) because there was something there that might help us find Henry. In fact, I tried to shut out every other thought except for the fact that Henry was probably in danger and that Dracula's daughter was the only one who could help me find him.

I had been expecting a ruined castle with bats and shadowy corners, but instead we pulled up in front of a small cottage hidden among dense trees.

Bella dismounted but then paused in front of me. Her blue eyes pierced mine and for a second she looked almost awkward. "You are the first mortal I have allowed here for more than a hundred years," she said.

While I'm sure Henry would have known exactly what to say to that, I didn't, so I stayed quiet and did my best to show how honored I was by smiling.

The door of the cottage opened of its own accord before we got to it. I tried not to look too amazed. After all it was something I guessed I should expect when visiting a vampire's house. We went inside and Bella lit a lantern.

"No electricity up here," she said. "And I don't really need light to see by, but I don't think you'd appreciate being here in the dark."

I looked around in the dim golden light and saw a small room, with very little furniture—just a chest, an armchair and a side table—and not much else by way of decoration, except for a portrait of a stern-faced man with thick, dark eyebrows that hung above an empty fireplace.

Seeing my look, Bella held the lantern up and shone it on the face. "My father," she said.

I must admit I stared a bit—who wouldn't? This was an actual portrait of the real Count Dracula. It didn't look anything like Christopher Lee—and not in any way like the portrait that hung in Castle Bran. It did look at lot like the picture in Henry's book. Score for HH! In fact, despite being a bit severe, it was not an unpleasant face at all. No fangs in sight, and with a recognizable likeness to Bella. He looked powerful and demanding—as though he expected a lot. I felt like I wouldn't want to let him down if he were my dad.

She set the lantern down on a tabletop and crossed to the big brass-bound chest tucked into the corner of the room. It looked like the kind pirates would use to bury their treasure.

Bella was lifting an object wrapped in oilskin out of the chest. She laid it on the table next to the lantern and unrolled it. Inside was a very ancient-looking piece of parchment with a map drawn on it.

"This belonged to my father," said Bella. "He always kept it locked away in a secret place. I found it only a hundred years ago and I have never really examined it properly. But I remember that it shows places that are no longer found on modern maps.

She bent over the parchment, tracing the lines of rivers with her finger, murmuring the names of towns and villages aloud. Then she stopped, her finger resting on the only bit of the map that had color on it.

A place marked in red.

You didn't have to be a genius to guess it was written in blood. And the word?

SNAGOV

I looked closer. Next to it was a little clutch of buildings drawn with amazing detail. A village? But something else was marked there—a wandering path that lead to what looked like the entrance to a cave. Beside it was a tiny drawing of something that looked remarkably like the picture Henry had copied from the well at Castle Dracula.

A picture of the Snagov Beast.

As I stared at it I felt almost dizzy. My eyes

blurred and I thought the creature moved and grew larger. Then my sight cleared and it was once again just a few lines inked on crumbling parchment.

I looked at Bella. Her eyes were glazed, almost as if she'd given in to sadness. But it was gone a moment later, and she brightened again, tapping the map with a finger.

"Here is where I think we will find your friend. As I had thought, it is not so far from here."

"All right, then, let's go," I said, reaching for my pack. I was desperate to find Henry before it was too late. If he was in danger, I hope he knew I would be looking for him.

"Wait, there's something else," Bella said. She reached into a pocket of her leather outfit and pulled out a medallion on a broken chain.

"I wanted to show you this—I took it off one of those people who attacked you the other night."

As it hung before me I felt dizzy again. On

the medallion—which looked like gold—was a much larger picture of the beast from the map. The weird thing about it was that the more I looked at it, the less easy it was to see. The shape and form of the beast seemed to change as I stared. Did it have wings, or tentacles, or both? I honestly couldn't tell. I wished Henry Hunter were there to explain it all. But he wasn't—and that thought brought me back to earth with a bump.

"What do you think the Snagov Beast really is?" I asked.

"All I know is what my father told me, long ago. He didn't really explain it, just hinted that there was a creature who was the 'first'—the first vampire, that is. All those who came after, somehow came from it—including my father. He never told me what it was or where it might be found. But I remembered that he had this map and that he would never let me look at it. I did, of course, in the end, and I think it shows where we must go to find your friend."

She looked at me seriously. "I can only conclude from the medallion that those people we encountered are somehow connected to the Beast."

I had already guessed this, but her confirmation still shook me. I grabbed my pack and said, as firmly as I could, "Then we'd better get going. Every moment may put Henry in greater danger."

THE ORDER OF
THE DRAGON

For most of the journey to Snagov I just shut my eyes and tried not to think of the perilous cliffs that fell away into darkness on either side as we sped through the night. The only trouble was that every time I closed my eyes, all I could see was the outline of the Beast, writhing its tentacles (or whatever they were) in the air, and glaring at me with blood-red eyes.

It meant I was pretty happy when we finally screeched to a stop on the outskirts of the little town of Snagov. It was still dark, but I could see Bella glancing at the sky a couple of times. Dawn could not be that far off. The sooner we reached the cave and got under cover the better—before Bella got hit by the sun. And yes, I knew this meant we'd be closer to the Beast—but we'd also, I hoped, be closer to rescuing Henry.

Bella throttled the engine to a quieter level and wove her way quickly though the deserted narrow streets dotted with small red-roofed houses until we were out on the main road again. We passed the ruins of what must have once been a monastery, and I remembered again that Snagov was where Bella's father— Count Dracula—was buried. I glanced at Bella—she was staring at the ruins with a strange look in her eyes. I supposed that even a seven-hundred-year-old person must feel a bit sad near the grave of one of their parents— even if he was Vlad the Impaler.

The winding track led up into a range of mountains, growing steeper all the way. After a while even Bella's motorbike began to sound breathless, and as the terrain became too uneven for the bike's tires, she pulled over to the side of the road.

"We'll walk from here," she said, dismounting. As soon as I'd jumped off she hid the bike in a thick strand of bushes. I hoped we'd be able to find it again on the way back.

That's if we ever did come back.

We pressed on by foot, climbing always higher, scrambling over rough slopes. Having had very little sleep, I was struggling with exhaustion at this point, and several times I slipped. But Bella was looking

out for me at every turn, it seemed, and would grip my arm to stop me from falling down the mountainside. I realized that she could probably travel a lot more quickly than me—I was holding her up. But when I tried to suggest that she go on ahead of me she simply shook her head and continued to climb.

Finally she stopped. We'd arrived at a place where the rocks formed a natural shelf, and there before us was a narrow opening leading into darkness.

I remembered the words cast by the Transylvanian glass, back in Whitby:

In the cleft of the Mountain of the Worm is the Snagov Beast.

"What's this place called?" I asked, pretty much knowing what the answer would be.

As if she had read my mind, Bella spoke. "In English, this place is called the Mountain of the Worm." Then she held her finger to her lips, as if listening.

All I could hear, other than the wind, was my heart hammering.

"There are at least twenty people inside—maybe more," she said eventually.

"Can you hear Henry?"

She listened again. "No, I can't hear his voice. That doesn't mean he's not in there," she added as my shoulders slumped. "He may be asleep, or unconscious or simply out of range. Even my hearing has its limits."

I didn't much like the idea of Henry being unconscious, but I knew it was a possibility. We had to go in.

"We'd better get moving then," I said, heading towards the dark opening.

Bella held back my arm. "So impulsive! We need to go quietly. Try to make your big feet tread as softly as you can."

I tried not to look hurt. My feet aren't that large, though I suppose if you're a silent-stepping vampire all humans make a lot of noise. So I followed Bella into the crack in the rocks as quietly as I could, trying to remember all of Henry's lessons in surveillance—putting the weight on the balls of my feet rather than the heels, trying to breathe as quietly as possible.

We found ourselves in a high, narrow passage that looked as if someone had used a pickaxe to widen it. There was really only enough room for one person at a time, so we went in single file. A few minutes later we emerged into a much larger, darker space. I reached for my flashlight, about to flick the switch, when Bella knocked my hand aside.

"Do you want to tell the whole world we're here?" she hissed. "Silly boy! I can see well enough. Just stay close and I'll make sure you don't fall into any holes."

I was angry at myself for being so stupid, and began to follow Bella blindly, knowing only that I was in the middle of a cavern of some kind. The darkness pressed in on me like a thick curtain. Every sound we made (or should I say I made?) seemed to be magnified in the otherwise silent cave. But finally I began to hear other sounds—a kind of hollow booming—that I gradually realized was the voices of people echoing back from the cavernous walls.

They were chanting something. And

although I couldn't hear what it was, there was an ominous quality to it that spooked me. By now, some light was visible, and I no longer had to rely solely on Bella to guide me. The light got stronger, until we arrived at the entrance to another cave and brightness poured in, along with the sounds of chanting. And then it stopped. We heard a voice calling for silence.

Bella pressed a finger to her lips and laid down on her front, signaling for me to do the same.

We inched our way forward on our elbows until we could see into the cave. It was a smallish cavern and brightly lit by dozens of burning torches stuck into holes around the walls. The smoke rising from them gave everything a wavering quality that made the scene all the weirder.

There were maybe sixty people in there, and I remember thinking at the time that

they'd all obviously been watching too many horror movies, because they were dressed in long dark robes with hoods. I recognized the medallions they had around their necks— the same as the one Bella had shown me at her house. They were gathered in front of a big rock that formed a natural platform, on which stood a figure in a red robe—I suppose so you could tell he was the boss. He had his hood pulled down so I couldn't see his face, but there was something unsettlingly familiar about his voice.

"My friends," he said, "I speak to you in English because there are many here who have come from afar and do not know our tongue. The time has almost come when our work will be complete. The Great One will arise! He will make us all immortal! Then, we shall take our places in the world as leaders, as conquerors!"

His words didn't surprise me. Why is it these types always want to conquer everything?

I thought. I mean, if they actually got all the power, what would they do with it?

Meanwhile, there was a lot of chanting of "The Great One! He arises!" and that sort of thing. They sounded a bit like a football crowd, albeit an echoey one.

The hooded leader held up his hands. "Tonight we shall offer an interloper to the Great One. This offering will be the means of his awakening. His gratitude will be such that he will reward us all! The Order of the Dragon will be triumphant!"

So that was who they were. As Henry had told me, Dracula himself, Vlad Tepes, had belonged to an Order of the Dragon, back in the Middle Ages. But I thought that had been a kind of Knights of the Round Table thing, with a lot of guys running about waving swords. What were these people doing here now?

They were all still chanting, but I had stopped listening. I had a nasty feeling that by "interloper" the hooded guy meant Henry, and judging by Bella's expression she had reached the same conclusion. She pointed backwards and we withdrew from the cavern.

As soon as I thought it was safe to speak I whispered, "They mean Henry, don't they?"

Bella nodded grimly.

"And they're going to feed him to the beast thing, aren't they?"

"I'm afraid you may be right," she said in a very low voice.

"So what can we do?"

"We must see if we can discover where they are holding him. Then we will decide what to do."

I was glad that Bella was taking charge—she seemed so decisive—but before I could say anything more my ears were hit by a sudden outburst of shouting from the cave. We crawled back to our viewpoint and stared down at the scene.

"Well," I murmured—the noise in the cave

would no doubt cover up anything I said—"at least we don't have to go looking for him now."

There, looking a bit dazed, was Henry—held on the platform by two large men in robes. I recognized the main expression on his face—curiosity. Whereas most people in HH's situation would give in to fear, Henry was fascinated by everything going on around him.

At the sight of my friend, I was overwhelmed with both relief and concern that the worst might be yet to come.

The leader held up his hands for silence again.

"My friends," he bellowed, "the moment for which we have worked so long is almost upon us. Soon the Great One shall awaken, and this foolish enemy shall be the first to feel his anger and the first one upon whom he will feast."

Henry's eyes were darting about, probably looking for a way to escape, while everyone started shouting and cheering and jumping about again. The man on the platform pushed back the hood of his scarlet robe and spread his arms wide as if to embrace his followers.

Now I realized why his voice had seemed familiar.

It was Mr. Antonescu.

As I stared at our "guide" I got that funny, empty feeling in the pit of my stomach—you know, the kind of feeling you get when you've just heard your best friend got eaten by a tiger. I looked at Bella. She was staring at Mr. Antonescu with a very intent look. Then she said a few words in her own language, before switching to English.

"I know this man."

"Um, well, he was our guide . . ."

"Of course, I know that! But there is something about him. . . . Something from the past . . ."

For a second longer Bella stared at Mr. Antonescu, who was still directing the chants and cries of "The Great One!" like a conductor in an orchestra; then she snorted. "Never mind. There is no time for this. We must rescue your friend."

I was desperate to do the exact same thing, but as I looked at the crowd in the cavern—who all looked decidedly crazed—and the two hulking guys holding Henry, I didn't have much of an idea how to go about it.

Fortunately, Bella did.

"This is going to look a little weird," she warned, and before I could ask what she meant she began to change.

Her form wavered, right there before my eyes. For a moment she became transparent so that I could see the cavern though her; then she faded out entirely. In place of Bella was a plume of green-gray smoke, which began to drift away across the cavern over the heads of the chanting group. At the same time I heard, like an echo that was somehow inside my head, "Stay there. Be ready to run!"
It was Bella.

To be honest, I'm not sure

what else I could have done. Gone charging into the cave full of sweaty people in robes in the vague hope of not getting killed before I got to Henry? I don't think so!

So I stayed, watching and hoping. And, believe me, what happened then was pretty amazing.

The plume of smoke that was Bella hovered for a minute over the head of Mr. Antonescu, then descended onto the platform where the two hulking guys were holding on to Henry. The smoke suddenly grew still and, just as she had disappeared, there was Bella, solid and real. Everyone froze. The mob stopped cheering and stared. Bella, on the other hand, flowed into action right away. She grabbed the two big guys who were holding Henry and tossed them aside as if they weighed nothing.

As they flew through the air Bella picked Henry up. She tossed him over her shoulder like a sack of potatoes and jumped back down—right into the middle of the mob.

But the robed group had recovered from their surprise and went into full attack mode as soon as Bella landed. I've seen some pretty cool moves, although mostly on a film screen (well, who doesn't love a bit of Jackie Chan?), but nothing compared to this. Bella went though the mob like the hero of an action movie. A couple of them managed to land blows on her, but considering she was carrying Henry as well, most of them looked like they were made of cardboard. It helped, of course, that Bella was in full vampire mode by then, her face dead white except for her lips, which had turned a deep red, her blue eyes glaring like searchlights.

There were shouts of "Dracula" and "Nosferatu" (which Henry had already told me was the Romanian for 'vampire') and all of a sudden the crowd drew back. Only Mr. Antonescu seemed to be unaffected. He still

stood on his platform, his face a mask of rage—
far from the rather gloomy, uncommunicative
fellow of earlier.

"She is a traitor, an enemy of the Beast,"
he shouted above the din. "Destroy her!"

Meanwhile Bella had climbed like lightning
up to my hiding place, where she dumped
Henry unceremoniously on his feet.

"You okay?" I asked Henry.

"Just about," he answered, swaying a
bit. "Good to see you, Dolf—and you, Miss
Dracul. . . ."

Before the tide of Snagov worshippers could
chase her down, she turned and advanced on
them. It was clear they still weren't sure which
of them wanted to be the first to feel Bella's
wrath—or her teeth—and they recoiled,
backing off towards the platform, and their
leader.

But at this Mr. Antonescu's face became
even darker with anger. "Death to the traitor!"

he screamed. "Go after the enemy!"

Like sheep, the mob moved back again in our direction. They were obviously more in fear of their leader than they were of vampires.

"Time to go," said Bella quietly. "Follow me."

She took off at a sprint down the tunnel. Henry and I followed—though I could tell that he was still a bit unsteady on his feet from the way he kept tripping and skidding on the uneven ground. But he kept going somehow, though we had a hard time keeping up with Bella until I yelled, "Slow down a bit. We aren't vampires!"

It was pretty dark in the tunnel once the light from the cave had faded, and once again I had to rely on Bella. She led us off down a side passage that then branched several times. I guessed she was trying to lose our pursuers by taking turns they wouldn't even see. Finally she stopped so suddenly that Henry ran right into her.

"Where are we going?" he puffed.

"Away from those unpleasant people," Bella answered curtly.

"But who exactly are they?" I put in.

"An ancient society who worships the Beast," Bella said. "That much is clear." She looked around. "We should go further away from here. They are angry and will not give up until they have caught us."

I could hear distant shouts and cries—Bella was right.

"Well, let them try!" said Henry fiercely. "I can show them a thing or two. As for Mr. Antonescu . . ."

"There is something about him . . ." said Bella again, her eyes looking up to the ceiling in thought. "I just cannot remember."

"Where shall we go?" I asked, desperate to get out of the mob's way, no matter how many martial arts Henry was trained in. "Back outside or further in?"

"Further in is best," Bella said. "They will not expect us to go this way and besides . . ." She hesitated. "I think the only way to solve this is to find the Beast . . ."

I have to admit my heart sank then. As if we weren't in enough trouble already. Yet Bella was suggesting we go right into the lair of the Snagov Beast. It was fine for her—she couldn't be killed easily. I had a feeling we wouldn't be so lucky.

But I wasn't surprised at Henry's reaction. "That's the best idea I've heard all day," he said, nodding.

I could have been wrong but I thought I could see Bella smiling in the darkness.

"Follow me," she said.

AN ENCOUNTER WITH THE BEAST

Bella pulled out a piece of crystal from a pocket in her jacket as she led us further into the heart of the mountain. She held it cupped in her hand and it began to glow like a white-flamed candle. She was taking pity on us mortals, I thought—not that I was complaining.

I waited for Henry to remark on Bella's ability to light the way, but he'd been unusually silent since his rescue, and didn't seem to want to mention her gift. Instead, he asked Bella what she knew about the Snagov Beast.

"I already told Dolf—not much," Bella said in an annoyed tone, any hint of a smile long gone. "My father mentioned it and I have heard rumors of its existence. It is said that it was the first vampire creature to appear anywhere in the world. Some say it came from another world. Even my own kind are afraid of it, and some believe it is so powerful not even we could stand against it."

What? I had started to think that with Bella we'd be constantly protected. Now I tried to calm my rising panic.

Henry seemed unconcerned.

"The Harkness papers suggest that others have seen it more recently," he said. "And the Order of the Dragon gave me the impression they are expecting it to wake up any day."

"Did you find out more about who they are?" I asked, intrigued despite myself.

"A secret society," said Henry. "I think

they've been around for quite some time. They've been trying to locate the Snagov Beast for a hundred years at least. They're made up of people from all over the world," Henry went on. "I heard at least six different languages."

"What will happen if it they manage to wake up the Beast?" I blurted out.

"I expect it will arise from within this mountain and start destroying everything in its path," said Bella.

It was almost worse than my crazed imagination had feared. "And you still think it's a good idea to go and find it?"

"Come on, Dolf," Henry said. "Just think about it. This is probably the oldest vampire ever. It's what we came here for. I can't wait to see it."

I knew it was the whole purpose of this particular adventure, but unlike Henry, I could have easily waited—I couldn't help worrying that we were far out of our depth here, even by Henry Hunter standards. But I didn't say any more, and just trudged on down the seemingly endless tunnels, following Henry and Bella.

The air was getting warmer, I realized, and a smell that made my eyes water began to pervade the tunnels. Think of the nastiest, most puke-inducing thing you've ever smelled, multiply it by ten, and you'll have an idea what it was like.

Neither Henry nor Bella seemed concerned. *Perhaps vampires have no sense of smell*, I wondered. Henry just sniffed the air deeply and declared that he thought the Beast must be somewhere in the vicinity.

With Bella still lighting the way, the tunnel took a sudden plunge downwards and we found ourselves at the entrance to a new cavern. It was smaller than the Order of the Dragon's meeting place, but a lot more impressive. The high, vaulted walls were

semi-transparent, behind which moved what looked like molten rock—"magma" was the word Henry used later. We never found out how the chamber was formed, though my guess was that the Beast had somehow tunneled into the mountain and created a place where it could sleep and be warmed by the fires of the earth itself. In any case, at that moment, none of us cared too much—because in the middle of the cavern was a flat-topped outcrop of rock. And on it lay the Snagov Beast.

My first thought was that it was smaller than I'd imagined—about twelve yards long—and its skin was whitish. It was fat and slimy, like a very big slug, and the stink now we were close was even worse—think of maggoty meat or vegetables that have been left out in the sun for weeks. A fringe of squirmy tentacles surrounded its mouth, between which were plenty of sharp, pointy teeth. And it had a dragon-like tail with barbs all along it—

ending with four especially nasty-looking spikes at the tip.

But the most frightening thing of all was its eyes. It had two sets: a pair at the front, and a pair more than halfway down its back. They were open, red, and gleaming and they were looking straight at us.

The Snagov Beast was awake. And it looked hungry.

I wondered whether it had either just woken up, or was naturally slow on the uptake, because it continued to stare at us for another minute before it began to unfurl its barbed tail. Then it suddenly came at us a lot quicker than its previous movements had suggested it capable of—lightning fast.

I think I let out a yell, but as I turned to run back down the tunnel I realized that neither Henry nor Bella was following me, so I twisted back. They were both staring at the Beast—but neither of their expressions conveyed any form of horror. Henry's face was alight—he looked just about as excited as I'd ever seen him—while Bella had a strange, faraway look in her eyes.

"The first one," she said quietly, as if to herself. "The origin of my kind. I cannot believe I am seeing it."

Finally I just yelled as loudly as I could, "We have to get out of here!"

At this both Henry and Bella came out of their trances, partly at least because the beast's tail was now perilously close to us, flicking and swiping, and all three of us fled back along the tunnel. After a few hundred yards Bella stopped, and held up her hand in a gesture of quiet. We listened for the sounds of pursuit.

Silence.

Then Henry said, "We have to go back."

I stared at him. Was he serious? My look must have said it all.

"Someone has to face the Beast—we have to find a way to stop it," Henry stated.

"You are right," Bella replied with a nod. "I was blinded by the shock of seeing it. But if it gets free there is no knowing what horror it will bring about."

She turned away and began to walk back down the tunnel—towards the Beast's lair.

Henry looked at me. He was about as serious as I've ever seen him. I knew then that this was our fate. This was where our adventure had led us.

"Ready, Dolf?" he asked.

"If you say so," I answered. There was no way that I was going to let Henry down now, not after all we'd been through.

"Good chap," he said, beaming.

With Bella already out of sight, Henry and I strode back down the tunnel. It was then that we heard a cry. Bella! We looked at each other and broke into a run, emerging at the entrance just in time to see Dracula's daughter launch herself at the beast.

She seemed to hang in the air for a moment before hurtling towards the slug-like body of the creature. But quick as she was, the beast was quicker. It swung its huge tail like it was a tennis racquet and Bella the ball. *Smack!* She flew across the cavern and hit the wall with a sickening thud. She slid down the side of the cave and lay still. The Beast began to heave its sagging bulk across the cavern towards her.

While I stood frozen in horror, Henry leapt into action. He picked up the nearest large stone and threw it right at the beast. Maybe it was luck, but he managed to hit one of the large red eyes on the creature's back. If Henry's intention was to distract it from Bella, he succeeded. It recoiled and hissed like a giant angry snake. At us. Henry and I had now become its number one targets.

You might be surprised to know that I've

never stood in the path of a charging rhino, or a maddened bull elephant, but I imagine it's a similar feeling to having several tons of angry vampire beast hurtling towards you. Not fun, I can tell you.

Both Henry and I turned to run, but the Snagov Beast was too quick for us. I felt a great slap on my back from the Beast's deadly tail, propelling me through the air and slamming me into the wall beside Bella.

Everything went dark.

I guess I was only unconscious for a minute, because when I came to, nothing much seemed to have changed. I pushed against the floor but struggled to sit up. My whole body ached in ways I'd never experienced and my legs just wouldn't work. I looked around—the first thing I saw was Henry. He lay on the ground a few yards away, like a bundle of rags on the floor. His head was turned towards me and there was a livid red mark on one of his cheeks emitting a dripping line of blood. His eyes were closed and I could make out only the faintest rise and fall of his chest.

My attention was taken by a shadow falling across us both. I couldn't help but look up—right into the nasty, slobbery face of the beast.

There was no mistaking the meaning in its maddened eyes and waving tentacles. I could imagine it thinking: *Got you.* And probably something like: *Dinner!* Or possibly just: *Yum!*

Just as I was beginning to wonder what it would feel like to be swallowed by that great mouth, the creature reared up with a long drawn-out hiss.

At first I thought it was just getting ready to strike—then I saw that there was something on its back. Bella! She'd stuck a long sharp object into one of the eyes on its back! The

sharpened stake somehow amused me, considering the whole vampire and stake thing, and the combination of that and the shock of being nearly eaten made me start to giggle uncontrollably.

Everything seemed to happen then at the same time. The Beast, hissing in pain, thrashed around until it managed to dislodge Bella from its back, and dragged itself in the direction of a second tunnel, opposite the one by which we had entered. Bella hit the ground, but rolled and regained her feet with all the gracefulness of a trained stunt person, and ran across to where Henry lay. He was beginning to stir and Bella helped him to stand.

I distinctly remember I was still laughing when a large group of the Snagov supporters club (aka The Order of the Dragon) burst into view. At which point I stopped as suddenly as if someone had thrown a bucket of cold water over me.

To say they looked mad would be an understatement. I suppose that if you had been waiting who knows how many years for a creature you worshipped to wake up, only to not just miss the event but to see it making a swift exit with a nasty wound, you would be furious as well. Not even their fear of Bella stopped them. They charged right at us, yelling all sorts of expletives.

By now I was on my feet and, though still a bit unsteady, I got ready to face our attackers. Henry joined me, looking pale and not entirely himself. Bella took one look at the advancing armada and hissed, "Quickly! The Beast must not get away. If it hides in the tunnels we will never find it. You have to follow it! Leave these . . . 'creatures' to me."

I must have been really caught up in the moment, because part of me wanted to stand and fight this group of mad idiots. Henry was hesitating too, but then Bella roared, "Go!"

and showed us her vampire teeth. We sprang into action.

It was at a sprint that we reached the tunnel entrance where the Beast had disappeared and headed into the darkness. I risked a quick glance back to see Bella being swallowed by a crowd of burly men, but I knew we had to press on. We had to hope Bella would be okay. The sounds of the fight faded away as we ran further. Somewhere ahead of us the Beast waited. All I could think of was that if Dracula's daughter could not stop the thing, how were two twelve-year-old boys going to do it? Then I remembered that one of the boys was Henry Hunter. I just hoped he had not finally met his match. . . .

One Bite Too Many

We staggered through the maze of tunnels. The heat, as well as the all-too-familiar stink of the Beast, became more and more intense. The tunnels would have been pitch-black, were it not for the trail of luminous slime the Beast left behind it, which gave off enough of a glow to prevent us bumping into the walls. It felt a bit like we were following a huge, rabid snail . . . with fangs!

Henry was uncharacteristically silent as we ran. Maybe he, like me, was thinking about Bella, wondering if she had survived the Order of the Dragon's attack. I kept reminding myself that she was, after all, a vampire. That meant she couldn't be killed, right? Unless, of course, someone got to her with a sharp stake.

"Dolf, is it my imagination, or is it getting lighter up ahead?" Henry asked, pulling at my sleeve to interrupt my gloomy reverie.

I peered into the intense darkness of the tunnel. I might as well have been staring at a solid wall.

"Not so that you'd notice," I said.

But as I strained my eyes to see where we were going, I realized I did notice a slight lessening of the gloom. But it wasn't the Beast's trail that was brightening. I turned to look at HH. He was this new source of illumination! It wasn't that he was truly glowing—not like something out of a sci-fi movie. More of a dim buzz of light, so I could see him outlined against the dark.

I was about to mention this when Henry stopped suddenly. I could definitely see his head tilted to one side, listening.

"Can you hear that?" Henry whispered.

But I couldn't hear anything except my own heart.

"I think the beast is just up ahead," Henry hissed. "I can hear it breathing . . ."

I frowned and listened harder, wondering if my encounter with the cavern wall had had more of an effect than I'd first thought. Was I going deaf?

"Come on," said Henry. "And try not to breathe so loudly, Dolf. We don't want to scare it."

While I was still contemplating the completely crazy idea that we might scare the nastiest, most terrifying creature I had ever encountered in my life (at least until that moment, anyway), Henry dropped to a crawl and began to inch his way forward.

Trying to control my (apparently) noisy breathing, I followed.

The tunnel made a sudden bend to the right, and there ahead was an arched entrance outlined by a dim, reddish glow. Soon we were able to look down into another cavern, similar to the one where we had first seen the creature, only smaller. There, crouched in a natural bowl of rock, was the Snagov Beast. It had not grown any more handsome or friendly looking. The wound in its eye leaked something yellow and disgusting, and had obviously not improved its temper.

Like the larger cavern, the walls were semi-transparent, and behind them moved the hot, restless magma that kept the beast warm and the cavern dimly lit.

The heat was so great that it was a struggle to breathe, the hot air seeming to press in on my lungs. "Okay. We've found our favorite monster. What now?" I whispered.

Before Henry could come back with some witty reply we both jumped out of our skins. A hand touched each of us on the back. I'm afraid I let out a bit of a yelp, too, and I have no idea how Henry kept quiet—I wished I had his level of self-control!

Both of us spun round—to see Bella grinning at us out of the darkness. She looked a bit battered, her spiky hair distinctly ruffled, but actually almost as calm and self-possessed as ever. Until, that was, she saw Henry's face—at which point she stopped smiling, leaned in very close, grabbed his chin and turned it into the light.

It wasn't very bright in there, of course, but even I saw what Bella had seen. Henry's eyes were glowing. This time the comparison was easy: they looked the way a cat's do when you shine a light on them—with a kind of spooky reflection. They were also bright blue. The same blue as Bella's eyes . . .

It was then that I noticed some other things. The livid mark on Henry's cheek had gone and he looked somehow... well ... different. His face was more angular, his cheekbones sharper and his teeth—there was just no other way of putting it—his teeth were a lot more pointed.

Everything fell into place. Together with Henry's sharpened sight and hearing there was only one conclusion: Henry Hunter was becoming a vampire! I had come to expect the unexpected, but this was on a whole other level.

"The Beast. It bit you?" demanded Bella.

"Not exactly bit," answered Henry, always one for getting the specifics right. "But I think those tail-barbs hit me. I felt it on my cheek ..." He put up a hand and touched the place where the nasty mark had been, then it crept to his mouth and I saw him exploring, very gingerly, his altered set of teeth. His eyes grew wider. It was one of the few times I've seen Henry genuinely surprised.

Bella pulled us both away from the entrance to the Beast's lair.

"How do you feel?" she asked Henry. Her tone was light, as if she was more curious than concerned.

Henry didn't answer immediately, and I could see he was trying to process this new information. Then he managed, "I feel . . . stronger. Like I could push over a house with one hand." Suddenly he was grinning, showing rather more of those pointy teeth than I felt was necessary. "I feel . . . great," he announced.

There was an awkward silence. None of us seemed to want to look the other in the eyes.

Then Bella said, "I am sorry, Henry." It was the first time she had used his name like that, rather than referring to us both as "silly boys."

"Thanks, but I'm not sorry at all," said

Henry, clearly already at ease with his new form. "I've never felt so alive, or so powerful. In fact, I'm really ready to take another crack at the Beast. How about it? Let's show it that it can't mess with us!"

Bella stared at Henry with a very strange look in her bright, glowing eyes. Then slowly, as if she was not really used to doing so, she really smiled. (Two sets of pointy teeth, I thought. Enough now.) She produced from somewhere in her leather outfit two long, thin knives. She passed one to Henry, who tested its weight and grunted in appreciation.

He and Bella looked up at me, and, as if being vampires allowed them to act as one, said in unison, "Wait here, Dolf. Keep out of sight."

I didn't need to be told twice, but I also didn't want to miss the climax to this adventure completely, not after everything that had happened, so I went with them as far as the archway, where I crouched down. I had a grandstand view.

You know those classic movies where the hero or heroine takes on a prehistoric monster or something nasty from the bottom of the sea? Like Godzilla, maybe? Usually, the monster in question does a lot of roaring and thrashing about, often demolishing buildings in the process, until it is finally dispatched by the hero. The difference here was that in the matter of Henry Hunter and Bella Dracul versus the Snagov Beast, there was very little sound at all. A bit of grunting, a fair amount of thrashing about, but very little roaring.

They both took off and literally flew across the space to land on the Beast—Henry at the head, Bella on the monstrous tail. I think it was more surprised than anything. They took advantage of this by hacking away at it with those long, thin knives.

Then they jumped and flew, attacking like a precision gymnast duo, as though they had worked out every move beforehand. It was clearly some kind of vampire thing, each knowing what the other's next move would be before they actually made it.

They were so dominant at first that I thought the battle was going to be over quickly. But after a few minutes the Beast regained its senses.

Then, above all else, I could hear the sound of the beast's tail hitting the wall with a kind of nasty wet-fish slapping sound, and the clunk as either Henry or Bella flew through the air and bounced off the walls of the cavern.

The Beast might have been ancient, and not long woken from a several-hundred-year sleep, but it was also immensely strong and very, very angry with its assailants.

Henry and Bella were still managing to land on the Beast's back and attack it with their knives. But no matter how many wounds they inflicted, the Beast was unaffected. I

watched the wounds close up in a matter of seconds, leaving not a mark. At the same time, the beast seemed to be getting faster. Its massive tail flicked this way and that, bouncing Bella and Henry off the walls like tennis balls.

Then it hit me. The Beast couldn't be killed. Any more than Bella (or, I suppose, Henry too now) could. It was a vampire. And not just any vampire, but the first vampire— and undoubtedly the strongest.

In other words: stalemate.

The same thought must have occurred to Henry and Bella, because after about five minutes of battle they both jumped clear, running up the walls of the cavern (which freaked me out more than the flying did) to where I crouched.

Neither of them was even out of breath, and the light of battle quite literally blazed in their eyes.

"We aren't going to be able to kill it," said Henry.

"But we cannot let it go free," said Bella. "The results would be terrible. It could turn everyone in the world into vampires."

I tried to process that thought, quickly realizing that I would be at the front of the line of those with new pointy teeth. Meanwhile Henry was doing what Henry always does best: thinking.

"If we can't kill it we have to make sure it can't get out of here," he said.

"How would you suggest we do that?" demanded Bella, hands on hips. "Or do you happen to have a few explosives in your pocket?"

For a second I wondered if Henry did. After all, one of his (admittedly non-original) mottos was: Always be prepared.

"No, I don't," he said, frowning in thought. "But there might be a way. . . ."

He turned back towards the cavern. The Beast was lying still, both pairs of eyes open (the wounded one seemed to have healed already), watchful for the next attack. But Henry wasn't looking at the Beast. He was staring up at the roof and walls of the cavern, where the trapped magma moved sluggishly.

Bella followed his gaze. Then they looked at each other and Henry grinned.

"Hot rocks!" he shouted.

For a second I wondered if Henry had finally really gone mad, but he was already explaining. "If rocks are chilled enough for ice to form inside them, and then you heat them up, they literally explode. . . ."

"But," I said, my brain struggling to keep up, "aren't these rocks hot already?"

"Exactly." Henry beamed. "But if we make them cold, they'll heat up again very quickly and . . . boom!"

"Um, okay . . . I guess. But how will we

make them cold? I haven't seen a fridge or freezer in our travels inside this cave."

"No need," replied Henry. "Is there, Bella?"

Bella shook her head.

When I rubbed my forehead, trying my best to work out what they meant, Henry took pity on me. "Vampires can bring the temperature of anything down. It's why you feel a chill when a vampire enters a room." His brow creased. "Although I'm not really sure why...."

"It's so that we can preserve our bodies for long periods if we are unable to feed," said Bella. She didn't say "Silly boy," but I could tell she was thinking it.

I realized I knew even less about vampires than I'd thought. "Okay," I said. "So how do you do that?"

"Well," said Henry, looking down into the pit where the Beast crouched, waiting for another assault. "I'm afraid we'll need you to distract it, Dolf, to give Bella and me the chance to get over there and cool down the rock face. After that—get ready to run!"

I hadn't for a second thought they'd need me—a mere mortal—to help with the plan, and if I'm honest, I didn't much like the sound of it. I realized that since neither Henry nor Bella could really be harmed by the beast, they didn't understand what it was like to be truly scared of it. All I needed was a blow from that spiny tail and . . . hello, Adolphus the vampire! But Henry and Bella were already on the move, so I had no time to question it.

As I was so used to, even at that early point in our adventures, I did what Henry asked and ran to the entrance to the cavern. I began to dance about, waving my arms and shouting rude things at the Beast.

For a moment it seemed not to notice. Then, with frightening speed, it struck. I had just enough time to jump back as its huge tail, with its deadly barbs, only just missed me. The Snagov Beast lumbered into full motion, and I yelled as it headed straight towards the tunnel mouth—and yours truly!

As soon as the beast's attention was taken, Henry and Bella launched themselves into the air, flying across the roof of the cavern towards the wall furthest away from the beast. They put both their hands flat against the heated rock face, and at once a network of icy lines spread out across the stone like frost patterns on a window. I remember being both impressed and horrified by their obvious powers.

But although my friends were playing their parts with ease, I clearly wasn't doing my job well enough—the Beast had swung its huge bulk away from me and began to slither towards the furthest wall. As the waves of ice crystals spread from the four hands pressed against the wall, the cavern emitted

a grinding sound. Job done, Henry and Bella sprang back across the cavern just as the Beast's tail narrowly missed them. It let out a gurgling hiss of fury and turned quickly to follow us.

But it was too late. As the icy rock face heated up again, cracks split the walls and sharp bangs rang out as the stones exploded. I felt Henry and Bella grab my arms, pulling me away from the cavern and down the network of tunnels at tremendous speed, my feet not even touching the ground. Behind us we heard a massive roar. I happily imagined the walls collapsing inwards, releasing the trapped magma to overwhelm the beast.

Perhaps it did happen just as I'd hoped, as we were all suddenly hit by an enormous wave of hot air, propelling us onward though the tunnels. Not something I would think every day, but I was glad I had two vampires holding on to me, because I would otherwise have been shattered into rather small pieces by the sheer power of the blast. Instead their bodies shielded me and I could hardly believe it when seconds later we were standing outside, at the entrance to the tunnels, shaken but (as far as I could tell) unharmed.

I took my first breath of clean, fresh air since we'd entered the Beast's lair. It was just about the most wonderful thing ever. Better even than double chocolate fudge ice cream.

Then I looked around and saw that our troubles were not over at all.

ALMOST THE END OF THE STORY

It was still not quite dawn, which was just as well for Henry and Bella—but it wasn't that fact stopping us in our tracks. Facing us was a very angry crowd of the Order of the Dragon, many of them carrying flaming torches. Most of them appeared rather the worse for wear, and I saw many looking nervously at each other when they saw that Bella was still very much alive.

They were led by Mr. Antonescu, his

mustache bristling and the great scowl that he wore conveying his displeasure.

"What have you done?" bellowed our old guide.

"Made sure that the creature you worship will not be troubling anyone for a very long time," answered Bella.

Antonescu was silent for a moment, breathing heavily. Then he reached into his red robe and drew out a sharpened wooden stake.

"I should have done this long ago," he snarled.

As if they were all thinking with one brain, the whole bunch pulled stakes from their robes and surged towards us. I glanced at Henry and Bella, who were exchanging looks and grinning. Then they swung around and charged the collected members of the Order, whose mouths had dropped open as they realized they had not one but two vampires to deal with.

This time I was able to stand on the

sidelines, confident in the vampires' abilities, watching Henry and Bella take out the group with ease. After only a few minutes, most of our adversaries were lying in bruised heaps, groaning, and holding various parts of their bodies. Needless to say, not one pointy stake landed anywhere near either Bella or Harry. They left Mr. Antonescu until last, and then Henry nodded at Bella, who swept him up with one arm and threw him several yards into the air. He hit the ground and lay still.

Silence fell. Well, almost.

As I watched on, glancing over the bodies to make sure no one wanted to give us any more trouble, we heard a deep, groaning sound. I soon realized that it wasn't our attackers, but the mountain itself, which seemed to shiver for a moment, as if it were feeling the cold. Then a series of deep, echoing rumbles shook the ground.

"The tunnels are collapsing!" shouted

Henry, and suddenly everyone was staggering to their feet and moving away from the entrance to the Snagov Beast's lair as fast as they could.

Except for one.

Mr. Antonescu stood up, a trickle of blood running down his face from where he had fallen. He looked completely mad, his hair on end, his mustache bristling, his eyes staring. "The Great One!" he shouted, and began to run—into the open mouth of the tunnels.

Henry took a step forward, as though he was about to run after our old guide and drag him back, but Bella put a hand on his arm. "No," she said calmly. "Leave him to his fate."

And so the three of us watched motionless as Mr. Antonescu vanished from sight into the darkness, still shouting the name of the beast. Almost immediately there came the loudest rumble of all, as the whole front of the mountain groaned and shifted, and boulders the size of

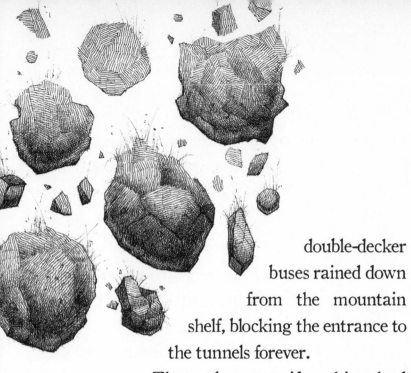

double-decker
buses rained down
from the mountain
shelf, blocking the entrance to
the tunnels forever.

Then, almost as if nothing had happened, the mountain was still again, sealing the Beast and its would-be master inside.

I wasn't surprised that without their leader, all the fight went out of the Order of the Dragon. They wandered off miserably into the night, and soon the three of us were all alone on the moonlit hillside.

"Do you think we killed it?" I asked.

Bella shrugged. "Who can say? It may well be immortal. But one thing is for sure: it will not be getting out of there any time soon."

"Well, that was a mission satisfactorily completed," Henry remarked.

"Except for one thing," I said. "You're a vampire." I wasn't entirely convinced that having a vampire for a best friend would be the ideal way to continue our adventures.

"Oh that," said Henry breezily. "You know, I actually quite like it. The strength, the power. . . . Think about it, Dolf—it could be quite useful." He smoothed his long hair back from his brow in a very well . . . vampirish . . . manner.

"Until you get hungry," Bella said. "I don't imagine that will go down too well when you get home."

I hadn't even thought of that, I realized. "Bella's right—what will you do when we get back to St Grimbold's? Start biting people?"

Henry's eyes grew serious—he actually looked worried. I think he'd been enjoying what it felt like to be a vampire without considering any of the practical side of things.

Meanwhile an idea started to form in my mind, something that might just save Henry. A thought so crazy that I almost didn't dare voice it.

"Um . . . this is going to sound a bit mad," I started. Two pairs of bright blue eyes turned towards me and I felt my mouth go dry. "Well, you know how much I like vampire stories. . . ."

Henry nodded, never taking his eyes off me. Bella stared with something like a smile.

"Well, it's just that I remember reading that for one day after someone gets bitten they can be returned to normal."

Henry turned to Bella. "Is that true?" he asked.

"Yes," replied the vampire girl slowly. "If another vampire bites you in that time, you will go back to being just a silly boy again."

Henry chose to ignore the jibe. "Another

vampire," he said, suddenly grinning. "Wonder where I'd find one of those?"

Bella relaxed her stern features. "Is that really what you wish?" she asked.

I held my breath. I knew Henry must be thinking of how amazing it was to be a vampire. And also that living forever (providing he never encountered someone with a pointy stake) could be very useful for someone with Henry's passion for strange bits of knowledge and investigating weird things.

Henry hesitated for at least a minute, during which time I tried to calm my rising concern that my best friend was going to remain a vampire. I couldn't imagine it'd mean the end to our adventures, but it would definitely make them a whole lot different.

Then Henry grinned. "I suppose it could get a bit inconvenient. I'd hate to wake up one night with a thirst and only you were around, Dolf. . . ."

I hadn't considered that! No way did I want to become a vampire too—I was quite happy as a boy, thank you very much.

Henry looked at Bella. "But didn't you tell us you'd given up drinking blood several hundred years ago?"

Bella shrugged. "I lied," she said, quite matter-of-factly. "I didn't want you to be afraid of me."

I suddenly realized I had become much less frightened of Bella since our first meeting. Even after this admission, I couldn't bring myself to truly worry that she was a threat.

"So . . . er . . . how do we do this?" said Henry.

"Roll up your sleeve," instructed Bella.

I have to admit I looked away. I heard the unmistakable sound of sharp teeth sinking into flesh, and Henry's quickly indrawn breath. Then, silence.

Finally I couldn't stand not knowing what

was happening and turned back. Henry was rolling down his shirt sleeve, covering two small puncture marks on his arm. Bella had withdrawn her fangs, but I noticed her licking her lips in a rather unsettling manner. I shuddered, but I was glad that Henry already looked more like my old friend. The bright blue glow had gone from his eyes, though he was still pale and his lips were redder than normal.

Now that I think about it, ever since his brief time as a vampire, Henry has seemed a bit paler than before. Later he confided in me that he still felt some of the strength he had gained—though he couldn't climb vertical rock faces at speed or fly across the room any more, which even I found a little disappointing. That could have come in useful.

Bella had her eyes fixed on Henry and it seemed to me that I saw a touch of sadness there—as though the thought of a fellow vampire to hang out with was something she'd have liked. Then she recovered, and glanced up at the sky, which was beginning to grow paler.

"I suppose I'd better take you back to your hotel, or you are bound to get lost. Hurry. There is just time before dawn."

So we stumbled down from the mountain, exhausted but victorious. At the bottom we

climbed aboard Bella's motorbike for the last time. It was a bit of a squeeze, but all three of us managed to perch on and behind the saddle.

Back at the hotel, which we seemed to have left days ago rather than just a few hours, Bella said goodbye. She could not have lingered even if she'd wanted, as dawn was just minutes away, but I suspected she was the kind who hates goodbyes anyway. I suppose if you are a seven-hundred-year-old vampire you probably get to do it more often than you'd like.

"Thanks for everything," Henry said. "Hope we get to see you again sometime."

"I think not," Bella answered, almost too quickly I thought, as if she couldn't afford to develop a friendship with two mere mortals. "Go home now, silly boys. And do not come back!" In spite of her harsh words I thought she was smiling—but I might have imagined it. Who can tell, with a vampire?

She climbed back aboard the bike and

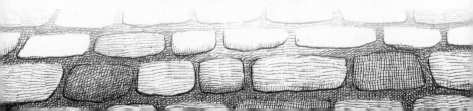

gunned the engine into life.

"Remember, we don't like visitors up here. It's not good for them—or for me."

Then she was gone, the red spot of her taillight vanishing into the early morning mist.

"Well," said Henry Hunter, "that's that. Time to go home, Dolf." His eyes looked thoughtful, as if he was a bit fed up, but if the reason had anything to do with Bella Dracul he never said a word to me about it.

It took us only a day to arrange our flights home, thanks to Henry's brilliant network of contacts. On the plane to England he was (for Henry) unusually quiet—though he still managed to explain more about vampire physiology than I really needed to know. Eventually I fell asleep while he was telling me how it felt to have your teeth suddenly grow longer.

I woke as we were landing. A car was waiting, ready to take us back to St. Grimbold's,

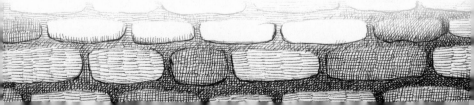

and a few hours later we were back in Henry's rooms at school.

He was already pasting the cutting from The *Unbelievable Times* into one of his big scrapbooks—he kept one from every expedition. Later he wrote a few notes and filed them all away neatly in old-fashioned box files with bright green labels. I know that he also wrote a long letter to Professor Killigrew at the British Museum, giving an edited account of our 'discoveries.' I imagine it's buried somewhere in a very deep vault.

As Henry worked on his scrapbook, I noticed a strange object on the desk in front of him. I was about to pick it up when I realized what it was—one of the barbs from the Snagov Beast's tail. I did a double-take and snatched my hand away as fast as I could.

"What did you bring that thing back for? Hasn't it got some kind of vampire-inducing venom in it?"

"It's just a souvenir," Henry said. "Besides, it might come in useful if I ever want to prove the existence of vampires."

There was just nothing to say to that, so I watched Henry wrap the barb very carefully in an old T-shirt and put it in an ornately carved box that he had picked up on an earlier adventure (I think it was The Case of the Haunted Tramp Steamer but can't be one hundred percent sure).

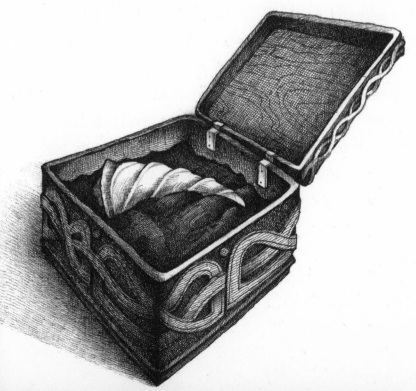

The box is in front of me now, along with a file labelled 'The Beast of Snagov.' Because, you see, the reason I'm documenting Henry's adventures is not just because they are great stories (which they are) but because HH is missing.

Yes, you read that right. Henry Hunter is missing. Not right after this adventure—it was over a year later. One minute he was there—the next he wasn't. (Well, maybe not quite as suddenly as that, but that's how it felt to me.)

He vanished on a perfectly ordinary morning in May, without leaving a note, and no one has seen him since. There was a huge search, but even the vast resources of the Hunter family failed to find so much as a trace. And now two years have passed, and pretty much everyone has given up looking—except for me.

Even Henry's parents, who came home as soon as they heard their son was missing, went back to South America eventually. But I can't stop thinking that Henry is still out there somewhere, probably being held in some dark, dank prison, and that just as he never gave up on me on any of our adventures—whether I was kidnapped, or tied up, or threatened by monsters—neither should I give up on him.

And that is why I'm telling some of our adventures, because I'm convinced that somewhere in these files are clues to Henry's whereabouts. Did you spot anything? If you did, please let me know, because I'm sure Henry needs my help.

And I wonder whether, like so many of the strange and wonderful objects Henry hunted down, the scary barb has anything to do with his disappearance. . . .

Perhaps, or perhaps not. But wherever Henry is right now, maybe he, or someone who can help, will read this account and get in touch. Because I'm not going to stop looking till I find him.

TO BE CONTINUED . . .

AUTHOR'S NOTE

This is the first "real" children's novel I have written, despite having begun many others over the years. It was a lot harder to write than I expected and quite a few people gave me encouragement to get it finished.

In particular, I would like to thank Dwina Murphy-Gibb for the many cups of coffee and fantastic suppers at the Sir Charles Napier, and for listening to me go on (and on) about Henry Hunter and Dolf, and always being interested.

To Ari Berk, doyen of all things mythic and folkloristic, for reading the first draft and being kind enough to tell me it was okay. (Part of the book was written in the little house we shared with our families in the Orkney Islands, and I hope that some of the fresh air and sea got in here somewhere.)

But my greatest thanks go, as always, to my family. To my wonderful wife Caitlín, for her tireless support when I was tearing my hair and declaring I would "never finish it," and to our son Emrys, who kindly read the manuscript when he was busy performing in *Guys and Dolls*, and put me right on some of the ways twelve-year-old boys think.

Thanks also to Mark Ryan for the suggestion about exploding rocks.

Thanks must go to Amanda Wood at Templar, who took a chance on this after only seeing a few pages, and then stuck by me when it looked for a while as if the book would never be published, and to my two resolute editors, Helen Boyle and Catherine Coe, who wisely ignored my rants and persuaded me to listen to them. This is a much better book than it would have been without them.

For those who like to know such things, most of the places mentioned in *Henry Hunter and the Beast of Snagov* are real. I have taken some liberties with descriptions of the various castles—though in several places I had in mind events that would happen there, only to find that they were exactly right for what I had imagined before I even saw the place. There are no caves near Snagov that I am aware of, but the local people still talk of "Dracula's Tomb" in the nearby monastery ruins.

For those who love vampire tales and can't get as far as Transylvania, I recommend a visit to the atmospheric town of Whitby, where Bram Stoker came in 1890 and where he gathered both locations and lore for his great novel of

Dracula. To the best of my knowledge there is no underground passage leading to the abbey ruins (though there could be), but all the rest of the details are as accurate as I could make them.

John Matthews,
Oxford, 2014

HENRY HUNTER

AND THE CURSED PIRATES

JOHN MATTHEWS

DON'T MISS OUT ON
DOLF AND HENRY'S
NEXT EXCITING
ADVENTURE IN...

HENRY HUNTER

AND THE
CURSED PIRATES